THE
HUNT THROUGH TIDAL VALLEY

MICHAEL COLE

SEVERED PRESS
HOBART TASMANIA

THE HUNT THROUGH TIDAL VALLEY

WWW.SEVEREDPRESS.COM

ISBN: 978-1-922323-78-1

CHAPTER 1

The night air was hot, as if it had recently been touched by the burning lights from the Death Flash. The moon was full. Hovering in the sky, it gazed down at the barren wasteland. Silver light reached down through a cloudless sky and touched the ruins of a country landscape.

It had been almost fifty years since the smoke cleared. There was hardly anybody still alive that remembered the war. The few that did couldn't even remember what it was about. The stories they told were of the blinding flashes that engulfed the world. Flames invaded the populations, killing millions in a hot instant, reducing humanity to a fragment of its former population. But Mankind did indeed survive, in his own way.

In fact, these days, it was all about survival.

A group of four watched from a small hill at a flickering campfire that slowly died down in the distance. They crouched low, being sure to be unseen. The hill provided plenty of obstacles to obscure any view of their position, as did all of the wasteland. All around them, they could see the remnants of old farmhouses and barns. Most of the houses had dissolved entirely, while the metal components rusted away in the dry dirt.

Their leader was Stahl. He was slightly taller than average, and well-built, considering their meager food supply. His black trousers had turned grey, and the rips in the knees exposed blistering skin. He scratched at a scar that creased over his bald head. Though over a year old, the damned wound never healed properly. And it always itched. He watched the camp carefully, as he had for about an hour now. There had been no movement of the individual they had been tracking. Beside the campfire was a sleeping bag resting several feet beside it. It was clearly full, the top of a head slightly protruding from the end, the edges tucked over the face.

He nodded to the others, signaling that it was time to move in.

His companions slowly branched out. To his right was Jac, a skinny bandit with a sickly complexion and thinning hair, despite being only thirty-three in age. Stahl grimaced as he watched Jac shaking with anticipation. It wasn't fear, but an eagerness to storm the campsite. Even now, with only one sleeping bag in sight, he watched in desperation that there was a female companion with the wanderer. It had been weeks since he last satisfied his primal urges.

"Jac," Stahl whispered. The thin-haired bandit looked back at him, his face containing a wide smile that exposed his crooked teeth.

"What?" he said, his twitching hand waving his crowbar side-to-side.

"Watch your jittering," Stahl hissed.

"There's only one," Jac whispered, his tone like that of a whining four-year-old. That smile disappeared as Stahl took a single step toward him aggressively, reaffirming his dominance over the group. It wasn't only the leader that moved; Carson did too. He stood with their only assault rifle tucked against his shoulder. It was fully loaded with thirty rounds. A squeeze of the trigger would empty that load in six seconds. Anyone caught in its path would be torn in half. He tilted the barrel toward Jac warningly. It wouldn't be the first time the man's jitters had cost them a prize. Hardly a week ago they were closing in on another camp. It should've been an easy target, as the leader of the camp was a sixty-year-old cripple. The prize would've been his two daughters. But the damn wire-haired bandit got too excited and moved in before Stahl gave the go ahead. As it turned out, that group had horses which resulted in a clean getaway. All thanks to Jac's unintentional warning that someone was coming to rob them.

His mouth still occasionally bled from where Stahl punched a tooth out. He swore that the next offense would result in a slow, painful death. Jac knew he meant it; he had done it before to a different offender.

Jac nodded his head. Carson turned the rifle barrel away from him. Standing next to Carson was the largest, and possibly most intimidating member of the group: Pepper. He had a face like burnt charcoal. His skin was a mix of black and grey, a result of being hit with smoldering embers thrown from a campfire. His skin was crusted and cracked, the only moisture coming from his eyes, which had miraculously survived the assault. Leather padding barely covered his muscular physique. Standing at over six feet, he held a spiked club, resembling a gladiator from ancient times.

"Okay, you know the drill," Stahl whispered as he moved around the small boulder. He drew a knife which he kept tucked in his belt loop. There was no need to explain to the group what their jobs were. They would advance on the camp. Pepper and Jac would move in on the sleeper and bludgeon him to death. If needed, Stahl would slice his throat, though that usually wasn't necessary. Carson, being the only one with a firearm, would keep watch. They didn't want to use the gun unless necessary, as ammo was hard to find in these parts. With only one occupant to eliminate, this should be an easy task.

"Go," Stahl whispered. The group broke into two pairs. Pepper and Carson took the left while Stahl and Jac took a curving path to the right.

They took long strides, keeping a pace that was barely below a run. They had to be careful. They didn't know much about their target other than he was alone, and that he was a *he*. Though not everyone carried firearms in the wasteland, some did, and Stahl could not be sure yet if this guy was armed.

The camp was between two large pointed rocks that, from a distance, almost resembled a teepee. The fire blushed between them, its orange glint flickering over the smooth inner sides. A metal skewer had been set up over it. It appeared that the camper had cooked himself some dinner before he settled down. Stahl could see the supply bag. He felt himself growing eager to loot it. It appeared to be full, with what, he didn't yet know. But that curiosity would come after a bloody minute.

He looked ahead. His eyes widened as he noticed Jac unknowingly closing in on the edge of a deep dark pit. He lunged and grabbed him by the back of the collar. He yanked back, the bandit giving him a brief frightened look. Stahl pointed. Jac looked back and saw the pit. It was at least fifteen feet deep, the walls flat and steep. It was a perfect trap for anything wandering at night. He gulped as he listened to the scurrying noises of the fang-toothed lizards that scurried around at the bottom. With jaws like piranhas, the flesh-eaters devoured anything that stumbled upon their habitat.

"Son of a bitch," Jac whispered.

"Watch yourself, you idiot," Stahl hissed. He noticed something at the edge of the pit. It was a large stick with a long wire at its tip, which protruded down into the pit. Undoubtedly it belonged to the camper. Stahl had to give the camper credit; it was a clever way of finding food in this area. In addition to all his supplies, Stahl would have to thieve his method of hunting as well.

He stopped and watched as Pepper and Carson closed in on the camp. Both groups were about thirty feet or so. Finally, Stahl raised his knife, signaling the attack.

Carson moved out to the center to provide cover with his rifle. The three bandits charged the campsite, one of them kicking over the fire along the way. Flaming embers scattered over the campsite as Jac and Pepper went to work on the sleeping man. The scar-faced brute struck first with his club, striking down just behind the neck. A loud crunching sound followed. He stomped down with his boot and pried the weapon loose and struck again.

Jac's movements were faster and more frantic, battering the victim's legs and ribs with his crowbar. He shrieked excitedly with each hit, bouncing up off his heels as he thumped the sleeping bag.

Stahl felt an initial excitement in their perfect execution. A small grin even creased his face. But that glee was short-lived. Something seemed off. There wasn't a single cry of pain. Not one writhing motion. No attempt to free himself of the entrapment and run away. No plea for mercy. Nothing.

One final thing he noticed; there was no blood.

Jac smacked the crowbar down one last time and spat. He and Pepper backed away, gazing at their kill.

"Didn't even get a squeal outta him," Jac said, feigning disappointment. His remark was followed by a chuckle. He ran the tip of the crowbar up over the ruffled sleeping bag, which was now gashed in numerous places. The mouth of it was still pulled over the victim's face, obscuring his identity. Jac could see the top of the head.

"Uncover him," Stahl ordered.

"I can do better than that!" Jac exclaimed. He moved in and kicked the head hard as though putting a football. He watched in stunned silence as the head detached from the body and flew several yards back. "What the hell?!"

"Holy shit, Pepper," Carson called out. He watched the head roll into the darkness then fell into laughter. "You must've hit him in the neck harder than you thought! Ripped his spine and meat completely. Took his whole head off!"

As they laughed, Stahl stepped away from the bag and followed it. It was lying several feet past the edge of the rocks. It was rounded in shape, trailing no blood from the stump. He picked it up, feeling no hair or skin. Just dry, hard wood. That 'head' was a log.

Stahl rushed back to the sleeping bag and slit it open with his knife. The flaps peeled outward, exposing several logs and weeds that had been stuffed inside it.

The laughter turned to silence.

"A decoy," Stahl looked around. "He decoyed us!"

"What? He's not here?" Carson yelled. Standing ten meters outside the camp, he was growing anxious. He turned to and fro, pointing his rifle into the night. A breeze stirred with a slight whistle, as though taunting him. He turned around, watching for movement of any kind.

He saw something twenty feet away. He placed his finger on the trigger and aimed. He tensed, ready to fire, then relaxed. After staring for another few seconds, he realized he was looking at another boulder. He turned and looked away, not noticing the figure that stepped out from behind it.

In the corner of his eye, he saw the silvery flicker of moonlight reflecting off the blade of a knife. It spiraled in midair; it was hurled at him with lightning speed. The weapon struck before he could react, its blade plunging through his neck. Carson spun, the nerves in his neck lighting up as though stung by a hundred hornets. He dropped the rifle, twisted in place, and dropped to the ground.

All at once, his three companions saw Carson fall. Blood spilled from his neck, soaking the ground. By the time they realized what happened, he was already dead, his hands gripping at the knife embedded in his neck.

They looked to the boulder, seeing the camper stepping out from his hiding place. Though faint, the orange glimmers from the fire were enough to reveal his gruff features. The man stood six feet tall. A muscular chest was covered in a black shirt and military-style vest. His face was scarred below the left cheekbone and above the right eye.

It was that morning when Pearce realized he was being tracked. Between the audible jittering of the skinny bandit and the fact that he circled back, allowing him to pick up his tracks, as well as theirs, it was obvious that four men were on his trail.

He had a keen sense of hearing. Even their whispers might as well have been shouted through a bullhorn. He even got to know their names as he waited behind the boulder. During their assault on his decoy, he was able to analyze their tactics, skill, and weapons. There was only one firearm, and the man holding it was now dead.

He took a step toward them, hands clenched into fists. They could see that he didn't hold a gun. He didn't need it. No sense in wasting bullets on filth that could be disposed of with handwork.

"Get him!" Stahl yelled. Jac raised his crowbar and charged Pearce, while Pepper moved around to the right to circle around him. Pearce watched the big man with the spiked club, then noticed the leader moving toward Carson's body. It was obvious he was going for the gun.

Jac closed the distance and brought the crowbar downward like an axe. A simple sidestep from Pearce caused the weapon to miss him entirely, its tip striking the dirt.

Pearce lunged, thrusting an elbow into Jac's nose. The bandit staggered back, his face now dripping blood. Pearce followed up with a hard punch to the jaw. Jac, his vision now hazy and his face throbbing, swung aimlessly. The crowbar stopped suddenly, locked in Pearce's grip. The loner pulled back and twisted, locking the attacker's arms out and overextending his posture.

Pepper started moving in, his club raised back over his shoulder. Pearce could see him coming from his left. He snapped a kick into Jac's gut, cracking ribs and eliminating any remaining control over the crowbar. In a parrying motion, he swung the bandit to his left, just as Pepper made his swing.

The spikes plunged into the back of the skinny bandit's neck. Jac's eyes opened wide, his final expression a combination of shock and sudden pain before the life left his body.

Pepper yanked back, the club dragging Jac's body like a ragdoll. He tugged on the weapon, trying to free it. A kick from Pearce struck him in the stomach, causing him to fold. Before he could right himself, his vision flashed as the crowbar was smashed over his brow. Pepper spun and hit the ground hard, his face now gushing blood.

With the crowbar still in hand, Pearce turned. The leader had reached Carson's body and was reaching down for the rifle. Pearce sprinted a few steps, shortening the distance. The rifle was now in the bandit's hands and he was starting to turn.

With all of his might, he flung the crowbar. It flipped end-over-end like a tomahawk several times before finding its target. Stahl stumbled back, feeling the rifle knocked free from his hands. He heard running feet coming toward him.

Stahl reached for his knife and turned to face the attacker. Pearce was just over a yard away and closing. Stahl thrust the knife, hoping to lodge the blade between his ribs. Strong hands clutched his wrist, twisting his arm outward. His joints ached as they were twisted beyond their limits, forcing his hand to loosen involuntarily, dropping the knife.

Pearce spun counterclockwise and threw the bandit over his shoulder. Stahl hit the ground face-first, feeling his teeth caving in upon impact. He scrambled on all fours then pushed up onto his feet. He lunged at the camper, throwing several jabs and punches, all of which were easily parried or simply avoided. Finally, he drew back and put all of his body weight into a right-handed haymaker. His fist came to a sudden stop.

With his left arm raised, Pearce blocked it. His other arm was already tucked back at his side, fingers clenched into a fist. In a laser-like motion, he thrust a straight punch into Stahl's center, blowing his air out. He pressed the attack as the enemy stumbled backward, connecting several more blows to his ribs and face, before finally knocking him on his back with a kick to the chest.

The world seemed to spin as Stahl scuttled back on his elbows and feet. What should have been a quick and easy pillage had turned into a disaster. He reached out for something, ANYTHING, to fight with. His hands found dirt and weeds. Finally, he felt the end of a small branch. It would have to do. He stood up and drew back, only to be knocked back down by a blow to the jaw.

Pepper seethed as he watched Stahl go down. He stood up, ignoring the throbbing in his head as he pried the club from Jac's corpse. He felt no huge loss. The bastard was annoying anyway. He did, however, feel a camaraderie with Stahl and Carson. One was dead and the other was now in danger. The circumstances of this clash were of no consideration. This had become personal, plain and simple.

Pearce saw the big man stand back up. He had taken a blow to the head from a crowbar and was still coming. Not only that, he still lifted the heavy club as though it were a twig. Pepper quickened his pace with each step. He gripped the club with both hands and lifted it high.

Pearce reached along his belt and grabbed his knife handle. Even in these circumstances, he was hesitant to use it. Wear and tear happened quickly, even to the sturdy blade of a tactical knife. But the situation called for it. He drew the knife, one side being a smooth cutting edge, the other side a chipped serrated edge.

Pepper bellowed as he swung the club. Pearce ducked, the weapon passing inches above his head. He slashed and moved, the blade finding the bandit's right thigh. Pepper roared out and felt his leg. His hand was immediately red with blood. No matter. He was no stranger to injury. This would just be another scar. It would serve as a reminder of a very satisfying kill.

Pearce straightened his stance as he waited for the bandit to make his move. Pepper took a breath and moved in again. He moved more patiently this time, cautious of the camper's fighting abilities and reflexes. He raised his club high overhead and came at him, appearing to bring it down. But Pearce noticed the slight twitch in his arm muscles as well as a pivot in his feet.

As he predicted, the bandit turned sideways and swung the club downward like a golf club, hoping to catch his opponent in the groin. Pearce threw a low kick, his heel connecting where Pepper's hands gripped the handle. The club fell from his grip and kicked up dirt as it hit the ground.

Pearce slashed again, this time catching Pepper in the shoulder. The bandit stumbled back, checked his wound, then gazed at Pearce with blazing eyes. He reached along his boot and pulled a knife of his own which had been tucked inside. It was a large blade, bigger than a steak knife. He waved it back and forth then slowly advanced.

"I'm gonna cook you over your own fire," he snarled. Pearce simply waited. With a flick of his wrist, he switched the grip on his knife, holding it reverse style. Pepper gradually moved in. Behind that snarling face was a small bit of apprehension; of which Pearce could detect.

Pepper yelled and thrust the knife out. Pearce stepped to the left, avoiding the blade. He slashed up, the blade connecting with Pepper's wrist. In a lightning-fast motion, Pearce lunged inward and slashed across Pepper's throat.

The lightheadedness came even before his brain registered the injury. The knife fell from his bloody hand as Pepper grasped his throat. Blood spilled down over his hands and chest and down his airway, suffocating him. He fell to his knees, spitting blood.

Stahl stood up on his knees and watched as Pepper's body faceplanted into the dirt. His entire group had been slaughtered. Only he survived. He stood up on wobbly legs as Pearce approached, knife still in hand. Pepper's blood trickled from its blade, the tip of which was now pointed at him.

"You prick," Stahl hissed. The camper never said a word. "You prick!" It was louder this time. "You think you're tough! Come on!" He raised his fists and took a step forward, only to scream in pain and drop after Pearce smashed his knee with a kick. Stahl writhed on the ground, his right leg bent backward at the knee. Clutching his leg, he gazed up helplessly at Pearce. "What?! You gonna kill me?!"

Pearce tilted his head and sheathed his knife. Stahl gulped as he noticed his hand brush by a holstered .357 revolver. In the madness, added by the fact that the wanderer was keen on fighting hand-to-hand, Stahl didn't even realize he carried a gun on him. It was the knowledge that the man didn't even bother to use it that frightened Stahl more than the weapon itself.

"What do you want?"

"Empty your pockets," Pearce said, his voice cold as ice. Stahl gazed back at him questioningly.

"Huh?"

Pearce reached for the knife. Stahl gulped and dug into his pockets. He gritted his teeth, feeling pain and humiliation. The robber was now being robbed. He pulled the few items he held and tossed them onto the dirt. There were a couple of small knives, some dried jerky, tape, a miniature flashlight, and a tin can containing tobacco.

"That's all," Stahl said. Pearce glanced down at the items then back at the bandit leader.

"Beat it," he said. Stahl went to stand up, only to collapse from the pain.

"But…my leg…"

Pearce grabbed a piece of lumber and chucked it down at him. Stahl took the hint. Using the wood as a brace, he stood up and hobbled out into the darkness. His leg throbbed as he kept going, the thin piece of branch cracking under his weight. He kept going, refusing to look back.

Suddenly, he was falling. It was as though the ground was swept up from under his feel like a rug. Ribs cracked as he landed belly-down. He groaned and rolled onto his back, his entire body now aching. Staring up, he noticed the moonlight glinting on the upper edges of the dirt walls. Stahl gasped.

The pit! He had fallen in the damn lizard pit.

He could hear tiny claws grazing the dirt. The pit was total darkness, preventing him from seeing the little creatures that shared the entrapment with him. They moved in circles, surrounding him. Then all at once, they struck. Piercing pain flooded his body as scissor-like jaws cut into his flesh. Stahl screamed and pushed up onto his knees, clawing at the dirt wall with stubby fingers which had been bitten off at the knuckles. The creatures climbed his body and dug their jaws into his face and neck. Ribbons of flesh were torn free, making way for rivers of blood.

Pearce dug through the bodies, pulling his throwing knife free from Carson's neck. He picked up the rifle. It was functional but extremely rusty. Luckily, the caliber matched that of the rifle he had hidden. He removed the magazine and patted down Carson's body, finding a second full magazine.

It was the only decent loot, as the other two thugs didn't have much to offer. Pearce walked to the boulder he hid behind and collected his rifle, then returned to his camp and rebuilt his fire. Sunrise would be in a few hours. He would sleep during that time before moving on. Roaming at night was always dangerous, as Stahl found out.

His sleeping bag was ruined. It was no huge loss. He balled it up and used it as a pillow as he laid back and munched on jerky. He watched the fire and gradually descended into a light sleep.

CHAPTER 2

The sun peeked over the smoky horizon, signaling the arrival of dawn. Its golden rays streaked across grey desert, exposing miles of charred soil and rock.

Pearce had awoken a half hour before sunrise. In that time, he had relieved his bladder and finished off the remainder of his fang-toothed lizard. He tended to his teeth with a twig, softening the end with his knife before rubbing it over each tooth. There were a few weed-like plants growing near the rocks. Their leaves were stringy, allowing Pearce to pull them apart into thin stands and use them as floss. By the time he was finished the sun had risen.

He stood up at the edge of camp and stared east into the wasteland. The area had recently been farmland during a more civilized time. There were a few rolling hills and the charred stumps where patches of trees had been before getting fried. A few new ones had sprouted but they were few and far between, hardly growing over seven feet due to lack of rain.

Between it all were the ravaged remains of metal vehicles, the solid components mixed in with the soil. Tractor parts, farming equipment…which hadn't been vaporized, and brick siding were scattered within the grey sand. The ground itself wasn't the smoothest; there were still remnants of the shockwaves created by the nuclear blasts. Some areas of ground had hardened into bizarre crest-shapes, like tidal waves frozen in motion.

There was a reason this part of the wasteland was referred to as Tidal Valley. Of all the inhospitable places, this was the worst. Bandits roamed freely. Mutations lurked around every corner. A traveler would have to watch his every step. On top of that, there was almost no water and very little vegetation. It seldom rained here, though some believed there was water deep below the ground. It was said that a few settlements had been formed to water farm the area, but Pearce had not seen any signs of them yet.

Somewhere out there, he would find what he was looking for. He looked to the weeds growing by the rocks. Growing inches away was a tiny plant comprised of two circular leaves, bright green in color. Between those leaves was a single purple flower. Not the right plant. The one he needed to find had bright red flower petals and the stem was said to be longer. However, the sight of the purple flower assured him that the one he needed might be here somewhere. He would just have to find it.

It was time to get a move-on.

Pearce checked his bag once more. The chemical processing equipment was undamaged from the bandits' meddling. The canisters and syringes were uncracked, and the dissolving solution was unspoiled. He went over his loot once more, stuffing the necessary items into his vest pockets and side pockets of his black cargo pants. The clothes were holding up well, having been kept inside an underground bunker for several years. The owner hadn't fared as well. He had been dying from an illness when Pearce stumbled upon his bunker. The illness was like a parasite, the germs feeding off the cells until the host was a dry husk of what he once was. And when Pearce met him, he was almost at that state; a living skeleton.

He felt a sudden squeeze in his lungs. Pearce leaned over and coughed violently. Scarlet dots trickled the dull grey ground in front of him. It was as though the memory of the old prepper had triggered the symptom of the same illness that tormented him. It was still in its early stages but it was a harsh reminder of Pearce's mortality. Unless he found the Red Flower, his body would gradually break down as though he had cancer. He predicted he had a year at most; seven months of which he'd be well enough to fend for himself.

The loner collected his rifle. It was a Dicer Model Six, a weapon developed during mankind's brief resurgence after the war. It held thirty-round magazines, of which he now had eight. To an amateur, it may seem like a lot. But Pearce understood that when ammo was used, it went quickly. Hitting a moving target that shot back at you was much different than shooting paper targets.

He double-checked his revolver as well. The six cylinders were loaded. He had two speed-loaders ready, and three other bullets that he carried in his pocket. Twenty-one .357 caliber bullets. He had recently stripped and oiled the rifle. Functional weapons were extremely important out here in the dry wasteland. There was nothing but danger out here.

Bandits roamed the landscape, looking for wanderers like himself. But bandits were the least of his worries.

Pearce glanced at the lizard pit, where the bandit leader had met his fate. He could hear the scaly critters scurrying about at the bottom. Those creatures were just one of many mutations that roamed the continent. It was like living in prehistoric times. Monsters, some as large as houses, searched nonstop for anything to feast on. None of these creatures feared humans or the weapons they carried. Pearce had already seen reptilian footprints as wide as his chest and signs of large insects.

Unfortunately, it was the only area where the rare Red Flower was said to grow. At least, that's what he was told. The sooner he found what he was looking for, the sooner he could leave.

Pearce walked eastward, keeping his rifle pointed low.

CHAPTER 3

His boots crunched over three miles of ground before Pearce found his first hindrance of the day. A twelve-foot lizard dragged its belly roughly a thousand feet out. He first heard its belly grinding against the earth, then the sounds of its claws dragging it along. Its jaws were crocodilian, almost a meter long. Serrated teeth, like those of a great white shark, lined those jaws. Its tail was spiked near the tip, its hide covered in thick scales. He could smell its horrid stench all the way from where he hid. He could see loose strands of material dangling from those teeth. Watching the creature as it moved, he realized those strands were from human clothing.

Pearce crouched low. With very slow movements, he crept toward a rock formation, keeping his rifle pointed at the lizard the whole time. It had not spotted him yet. It moved slowly, its spiked tail wiggling behind its trunk. Pearce slowly removed his pack and set it aside. He would easily find it if he had to retreat.

The lizard continued across the landscape, moving to his left.

Just keep going, you scaly prick, Pearce thought as he waited. He was on his belly now, keeping as low as possible as he army-crawled to the big rock. So far, it seemed he had gone unnoticed.

Then the damn symptom came. Pearce cupped his mouth. That damned cough! It was uncontrollable. There was not enough willpower in the universe to suppress it. He gagged himself with his palm, muffling the sound. Blood trickled onto his hand.

The lizard stopped. It remained motionless for several seconds as though its brain was processing something. It tilted its snout upward and sniffed.

The cough subsided. Pearce lifted his hand away, seeing the bits of blood on his palm. His eyes went back to the beast. It sniffed a few more times and turned its head in his direction. He cursed his illness. It seemed to be determined to kill him one way or another.

The lizard snarled. Suddenly, it drew its legs in and lifted its belly off the ground. Like a Komodo dragon, it sprinted toward the fresh meat. Pearce jumped to his feet and ran, pulling back on the cocking mechanism of his rifle. For having an awkward shape, the lizard ran fast. It opened its jaws and hissed loudly, as though informing its prey of its fate.

Pearce zigzagged between a few rocks before finding a tidal wave structure to prop himself up on. He grabbed the tip of the crest and hauled himself up. The creature lunged, snapping its jaws upward. Pearce rolled over his shoulders, his boots inches away from those jagged teeth. Frustrated, the creature started an attempt to climb, only to slide down the curved shape of the rock.

Pearce stood up and aimed his rifle down at its head. He glanced at the frame lever, making sure that the weapon was set to semi-auto, then fired a single shot. At that moment, the creature swung its head left. The bullet punched down into its shoulder, igniting its nerves and stirring it into a frenzy. The beast hissed and slashed violently. Its spiked tail vaulted high over its head, the barbs grazing the tip of the rock structure.

Pearce tried to aim for its head but the creature was moving too frantically. Finally, its claws sank deep into grooves already formed in the structure. It pulled itself up, snapping its teeth and twisting its body with lightning speed. Pearce fired again, trying to conserve his ammo. The creature's movements were nonstop, making a precise shot almost impossible. This time the bullet skidded across its snout. He fired twice more, the creature's thrashing movements causing the shots to strike it again in the shoulder and along its underside.

The creature lunged, jaws wide open. Pearce jumped back, his feet clearing the threat by inches. He backpedaled a few meters. The creature was now halfway over the ledge, its head still thrashing back and forth. Saliva sprayed from its jaws as they snapped repeatedly.

There was no more time to wait. He had moments before it would be up on the rock with him. With those teeth, he would be ripped in half on the first bite. He flipped the rifle lever, setting it to full auto, then aimed. A squeeze of the trigger sent a spray of bullets punching into the creature, shredding its neck and right shoulder. The creature hissed and writhed. It fell back over the crest, trailing streams of blood along the rock.

The loner set his rifle back to semi-auto as he returned to the ledge. The creature was still alive, bleeding profusely, but still growling and snapping its jaws. Though weakened, it was clearly still vicious. As was the way of the natural order, a wounded animal was often the deadliest. Putting it down with a knife would likely only result in him being torn apart. He pointed his rifle down. The thrashing movements had ended momentarily, allowing for easier aim. He lined the muzzle between the creature's eyes and squeezed the trigger.

Its skull split open, spilling red blood and brain matter onto the soil. It twitched and writhed before rolling to its side. Pearce watched its body spasm before settling motionless against the rock.

He drew in a deep breath and relaxed himself. The creature was dead. With that relief came an ounce of frustration. He had used half of his magazine—fifteen bullets; a commodity that was not easy to come by these days. But what was done was done. He waited, watching his surroundings in case the shot attracted any other unwanted visitors. He gazed back at the dead lizard. He thought briefly of cutting open its hide and taking some of the meat. Unfortunately, he had no way of storing it. At the very least, it would likely attract some of the other critters in the area. Keeping their bellies full meant they wouldn't be hunting him.

Pearce glanced around for another few seconds. So far, it appeared he was alone in the area. He glanced back. Same. Nothing but rocks and wasteland. He was about to step off the rock when he did a double-take over his shoulder. There was something back there, almost a quarter-mile behind him. It was a structure of some kind, newer and sturdier than the other ruins.

A fort, rather, what was left of a fort. It was made after the nuclear holocaust, though it hadn't fared well in the conflicts that followed during the Revival. He thought of ignoring it in favor of continuing his quest. Another thought hit at that moment: the fort *might* contain valuable supplies. Nonperishable foods left over from the Revival Wars. Water. Weapons. It was worth a look.

Pearce first doubled back and collected his pack, then returned to the site. During the journey, he checked every sliver of flora he came across, hoping to see those red petals with the green stripes. But there was nothing. He checked his canteen. There was only enough water in there to fill a coffee cup. It would not last.

He walked for ten minutes before arriving at the north wall of the structure. It was thirty feet long, equal to the size of the other three walls. The structure was made of solid brick that appeared to be made of black granite. The building had no roof. In fact, it appeared to be unfinished altogether. But it had certainly been used for its intended purpose: defense. Bullet holes marked the walls. There were several loopholes about four feet up intended for machine gun firing. Old sandbags were lined outside the structure, heavily deflated, their contents having spilled through tears in the bags. There were several crevices in the wall itself, their edges jagged and uneven, likely the result of dynamite or artillery fire.

As Pearce started to wander around the corner, his eyes caught a strange formation in the soil a hundred meters off to the east. With his rifle pointed, he carefully approached. The formation was circular in shape, the soil loose like beach sand, almost watery in texture. It was like a whirlpool of sand.

A sandpit.

He watched it carefully, waiting for any movement. Like the lizard pits, the sandpits were hazardous traps for anything not paying attention. They were like quicksand, waiting to swallow up anyone that came near it. However, it wasn't suffocation he was worried about. It was what *lived* in the sandpit. He had seen them before: huge arachnid creatures that waited for prey to draw near. Armed with huge claws, a rock-hard exoskeleton, and a deadly stinger, they waited patiently for unsuspecting prey. They could usually sense movement outside their hideout. If prey came close by but was too cautious of the pit, the arachnid would emerge and sting it. Some were known to grow as large as houses.

Pearce waited. Nothing emerged. He was possibly too far away, and that was fine by him. It meant there was enough distance between the pit and the building, which would enable him to continue exploring.

Pearce cautiously backed away and walked around the building to continue his inspection. The east wall was in similar condition as the south. There were breaches and cracks, but the wall still appeared sturdy. The north wall, however, was in complete shambles. The upper half of the wall had collapsed, forming black piles of granite all around. What remained standing of the wall was only about a meter high. Clearly, during whatever conflict had taken place here, this was the side that took the brunt of the assault.

It was clear that the invading force took advantage of the breach. Pearce climbed over the rubble and set foot inside. The interior walls were completely destroyed. Pearce could see the south wall from where he stood. Rubble was scattered all over the interior, some of which had dissolved to dust. The fort had been reduced to a giant granite box. It wouldn't even be viable as a shelter.

He stepped further in. There were no bodies to be seen. If there were, they were probably dragged out by carnivorous creatures and eaten. He glanced out, making sure there was no movement from the sandpits. There was none.

Moving around the remnants of walls, he searched for firearms and ammo. There was a metal chest near the northeast corner with a metal lock on the lid. He knelt down and tugged up on it. It was rusty but still holding strong. A good heavy blow would be enough to crack it open. Pearce looked around, found a large brick, and slammed it down on the lock, busting it open. After brushing away the gravel, he opened the chest.

There were miscellaneous items piled inside. At the top was a metal water canteen. He picked it up, feeling the water swishing inside. He unscrewed the cap and lifted the canteen to his lips, took a swig, and spat. To say it was stale would be putting it mildly. It tasted like liquid metal. Drinking this water would probably be more deadly than going thirsty.

Pearce tossed it aside and continued digging. He found an empty pistol. A Beretta. He pulled back on the slide. It only came back halfway. The metal creaked. This weapon had spent probably thirty years in this heat with no maintenance and cleaning. It'd be more suitable as a club at this point than a firearm. The magazine was empty anyway and he didn't see any spares lying around. There didn't appear to be anything else of value in the chest. Pearce shut it and looked around. Any weapons of value had probably been cleared out by other wanderers.

After walking through to the south wall, Pearce concluded there was nothing of value here. He had wasted his time. He turned back to go out the way he came, stepping over piles of rubble. His foot hit something metal. Pearce stopped and knelt to the floor. He brushed the rubble to the side, revealing a metal hatch in the floor. It was unlocked, the hatch itself slightly ajar.

He opened it and peered inside. A ladder led twelve feet down into a dark abyss. There was a stream of water below, moving to the west like a tiny river. He dug his flashlight from his bag and descended the ladder.

One of the few people in this period who had learned to read, he had learned of large waterlines that had been constructed before the nuclear war. They were designed to circulate water drained from rainstorms and ponds, keeping it fresh and safe to drink. Unlike sewers, it was only meant to supply drinking water, allowing for no waste to enter the stream. Pearce drew in a deep breath. It was significantly cooler down here, sparking an urge to set up camp. The air felt good in his lungs. He knelt down and took some water in his palm, then tasted it.

"Well shit," he muttered to himself. It was by far the freshest water he had tasted in years. He plunged his canteen into the stream and filled it to the brim. He stood up then shined his flashlight down the deep corridor. The walls were made of steel. There were pipes lining the ceiling attached to circular lamps. The electrical power had long been dead, casting the waterline in darkness. Whatever power source was keeping the stream in motion was either natural or simply didn't require much fuel, allowing it to run for decades. A generator perhaps. Either way, Pearce didn't care. He had what he wanted. And now, it was time to get going. He felt another stirring sensation in his lungs, meaning another coughing fit was on its way. Perhaps his estimation of his life expectancy was falling short.

He climbed the ladder and stepped out of the fort. He wandered out into the wasteland of Tidal Rock, continuing his search for the Red Flower.

CHAPTER 4

The loner continued another half mile east before finding a small hill to briefly rest. The area ahead was flat, allowing for a clear line of sight. He took his binoculars from his pack and scanned the surrounding area. It was one way of expanding his search, as he was only capable of covering so much ground on foot. He took a quick drink of his water then scanned the immediate area. The first order of life was survival. And to survive in this wasteland, you had to assume there was something behind every rock and crevice, waiting to kill you.

To the south was a cliff edge.

He confirmed there was nothing. He expanded his view further out. To the south was a patch of weeds. He zoomed in to the max. There was no flower in those weeds. Slowly, he panned to the west. Nothing.

That old prick was probably wasting my damn time. The sense of doubt started creeping into his mind. Even if he did find the Red Flower, if it even existed, he wasn't even sure it would work on curing his illness. After all, he hadn't heard of anyone that had tried it. For all he knew, it would probably make him sicker than he already was.

The Blood Virus was said to have claimed many lives, especially along the eastern coast. It was slow, torturous. Evil. It was like a ghostly being that slowly suffocated its victims. It hadn't reached the level of being a plague, though there were increasing accounts of people who had contracted it. So far, no cure had been invented. He repeatedly reminded himself that the Red Flower could cure anything, though his subconscious mind always added 'at least that's what they say.' It was a long shot but at this point he had nothing to lose.

He zoomed in on every rock and tree up ahead, saw nothing, then turned to his right. Again, he saw the cliff edge about a thousand yards out.

It was marred with rippling rock formations, like a raging sea. He panned lower. There was something about two hundred yards shy of the cliff. He first saw the green leaves then a glimpse of red.

Adrenaline started coursing through his veins. A breeze brushed over the wasteland, causing one of the green leaves to obscure his view of the flower. It didn't matter, he had seen enough. He grabbed his gear and hustled, being careful to watch for any sandpits along the way.

Pearce kneeled by the plant then immediately backed away. It was not a flower, but a red dandelion. Blood-colored thorns, poisonous to the touch, stuck out from its ball-shaped head.

The loner groaned in frustration. It was as though the wasteland was literally taunting him. He took a knife and slashed the deadly plant at its stem.

"Probably should've let the damn thing poison me," he muttered. "Be less miserable."

A gunshot echoed in the distance.

Pearce dropped to the ground and positioned his rifle. The shot was far away, originating somewhere to the south. Wherever it was, it was past the cliff. His ears picked up the sounds of commotion. He was not the target of that gunshot. He stood back up and cautiously approached the cliff. It was important that he assess any threat.

He knelt down between two large rocks, keeping himself obscured from the view below. There was a building down there, a large house. Behind it were drilling mechanisms near a large processing structure. It was a water farm.

There were people moving about. Pearce counted about a dozen, all dressed in ragged clothing. Some had spiked hair, while others were bald. The clothes were all black, mostly sleeveless. Pearce used the binoculars for a closer look.

Men on motorcycles drove in circles around the house, kicking up clouds of grey dust. Several others were on foot. Pearce counted three with firearms, though more were probably hidden from view. Up ahead, behind the motorcycle path were three empty buggies, each capable of carrying up to four people. Pearce zoomed in on the group. In the center was a man on his hands and knees. His clothes were different from the gang. Pearce surmised that he was the one who lived here. He was elderly, with a long white beard. He wore boots, overalls, and a long-sleeve shirt, all of which were tattered and covered in dust. He was quivering in pain, a hand placed to his ribs.

Pearce noticed other gang members shoving someone around. It was a female, roughly twenty years of age. She yelled, desperately fighting back until one of the thugs plowed a fist into her stomach, dropping her to her knees.

"Please!" the man's voice echoed. "I will gladly share with you! There is no need to—"

A kick to the ribs ended his plea. The old man rolled onto his back, groaning in pain.

"No need for what?" one of the thugs barked. The man grimaced, both hands covering his side.

"No need for violence," he said. "I don't believe in anybody going hungry or thirsty. I would share with you my supplies if you simply ask. You don't have to steal from me."

"How Christian of you," one of the other thugs said. He turned to his companions that groped at the young woman. "You hear that, boys?! He's willing to share!"

The men cheered, many of them converging on the woman. She screamed as one of them tore at her shirt, ripping it down at the collar.

"No!" the old man yelled. He started to stand but was knocked down by the same thug who kicked him. In moments the girl's clothes had been stripped away. Another punch to the stomach folded her over. One of the thugs took position behind her, his hands undoing the clasp of his pants.

"Please!" she screamed, only to be hit again.

"No, not my daughter!" the old man said. He struggled to get up but was quickly overpowered.

Pearce lowered the binoculars and looked away as the gang member began to satisfy his barbaric lust. His ears absorbed the echoes of the girl's screams. He contemplated his options. It was a hostile group. If he were to ever cross paths with them, they would surely attempt to rob him and leave his corpse to rot in the wasteland. He could launch a surprise assault and kill them, thus ridding any chance of a future threat.

However, the problem would be getting down there in time. Stealth would also be an issue. He was within firing range, though it would be difficult to pull off precise shots on moving targets at this distance.

He continued studying the cliff. It curved around to the south, where it continued for at least another mile. Further down, the rock wall slumped, allowing for easier passage. However, assuming the group was even planning to climb the easier elevation, they would have to travel significantly out of the way. The odds of running into these men were slim.

The old man cried out, watching the horror of the thugs taking turns on his naked daughter. There was laughter surrounding his screams. The gang took great pleasure in the misery they were inflicting. His mind briefly considered the ethics of standing aside. A voice in the back of his mind nagged him regarding the cruelty the landowners were experiencing.

"Not my concern," he told himself. He wasn't going to ignore the rules of survival. He chose to worry about himself. It was how he stayed alive up to this point. Avoid trouble whenever possible. Those who went looking for a fight were usually the first to die.

That stirring returned in his chest. He would have to cough soon. The realization prompted him to move. His coughs would likely attract attention he didn't want.

He kept low as he moved away from the ledge, straightening his stance when he was fifty paces pack. The pleas continued as well as cries of agony. Pearce put it out of his mind. He was not here to protect farmers from motorcycle gangs. He was here to focus on his own survival.

Pearce walked away, keeping an eye for movement. There was always some sort of danger lurking.

CHAPTER 5

The loner trekked north for another two miles. He had only found three trees and two bushes, all of which were withering. There had been no rain in over a month. Even those species which had grown accustomed to this climate were succumbing to the sun's abuse.

There was no sign of the flower.

Dusk was approaching. The sun's rays had streaked horizontally from the west. These were the hours that Pearce spent searching for a place to make camp. Usually he would have to go by a boulder, which would allow him to conceal the flames of a campfire. There was plenty of dried wood nearby, which he collected along the way.

He thought of doubling back to the fort. It would provide good cover for his flames. He thought of the sandpit, however. Those creatures sometimes came out at night to hunt if they hadn't eaten in a few days. Entrapping himself in that structure, three hundred feet from an arachnid nest didn't sit well with him.

Pearce continued south until he came across a series of tidal wave structures. He passed between them and found a small gorge in the earth. It was only a few feet deep, which was precisely what he needed. He checked around to make sure there were no sandpits nearby, then tossed his firewood into the pit. His stomach growled.

Before he would build a fire, he would find a lizard pit and set up a fishing line. He unpacked a coiled wire and strung it to the end of a branch and looped it. He had some leftover jerky that would serve as bait. First, he needed to find the pit. Pearce climbed out of the gulley and initiated his search.

After twenty minutes of walking, Pearce noticed a tiny gorge in the earth at the base of a small hill. Though not circular in shape, it was deep enough to serve as a habitat for the fang-tooth lizards.

He approached while tying the piece of jerky to the fishing line. Like on a fishing line, he had placed a hook in the loop, which would snag the prize once it took the bait.

"Mmmph!"

Pearce stopped. His hand went to his rifle, which was strapped over the back of his shoulder. His senses went on high alert. That was a human grunt he had just heard.

It happened again. He glanced around, seeing the burnt husk of a bus as well as a few other vehicles nearby. They were too far away for the sound to be coming from them. He approached the pit. He gripped the revolver handle and peeked over the ledge.

Twelve-inch long lizards scurried at the bottom, all looking up. Dangling just below the ledge was a boy. He was no older than nine years. His hair was curled and ragged, his face covered in dirt. He gripped a small extension below the ledge, his feet three feet above the hungry lizards below.

The boy didn't scream or even whine. He scraped his shoes into the wall in an attempt to push himself higher but failed to gain enough traction. Finally, he looked up and saw the loner standing above him.

Pearce stared at the boy for a moment, analyzing the situation. There was no gear on the ground beneath him, nor was there anything near the pit, which he thought to be odd. The pit, though obscured by numerous rocks, still should have been obvious enough to anyone traveling in the daytime. Unless the boy was just goofing around, of course, then fell in. Yet, it was strange that he didn't have any belongings with him. Not even a pocketknife.

The boy said nothing. He simply nudged his head back over his right shoulder. He did it three times before Pearce realized he was gesturing to the old school bus.

It was then that he heard leather boots thump against metal, followed by a muffled "shit!"

Pearce dropped his pack and stepped around the pit.

"When you throw someone in a pit, you usually don't let him hang over the side. Unless you're looking to attract attention," he spoke loudly. The bus door cracked and fell away, making way for the two men that hid inside. One stood six feet high and wore a bandanna over his face. The other had a similar build, with spiked gauntlets on his wrists. Their eyes narrowed at the loner.

The masked one looked to the other.

"Gotta give him credit," he chuckled.

"I admire someone who knows he has eyes on him," the one with the spiked gloves retorted.

"I know better than you think," Pearce growled. He stepped forward and turned to his left precisely as a third thug emerged from cover behind him. The thug was bald, his eyes red and dry, his teeth clenched as he swung a barbed chain. Pearce had already maneuvered, the chain passing inches from his face. He moved in as the thug swung back, catching his outstretched arm. The thug yelled as Pearce snapped it at the elbow. He followed through with a punch to the gut, blowing the thug's air out, before grabbing him by his sleeveless vest and throwing him over his shoulder.

He gagged as Pearce wrapped the chain around his neck and pulled, driving the barbs deep into his skin.

It took a minute for it to register for the other two thugs that their ambush had failed. By the time they charged, their companion had already been choked out. Pearce let go of him and gauged the distance between him and the other two. The spiked-wrist thug moved a few steps ahead of the other. He saw the fists clenching, followed by the right arm drawing back.

Pearce snapped his right foot out, catching the thug in the ribs with his heel. He fell back, nearly toppling over his companion with the mask. This one held a knife in his hand. He slashed inward and missed. He slashed outward, only to miss again as Pearce carefully predicted his movements. The thug thrust the knife out, hoping to drive the blade through his newfound enemy. Pearce stepped to the left, grabbed the thug by the wrist, and twisted counterclockwise, loosening the grip and prying the knife loose.

The thug staggered back as an elbow connected with his nose. Blood trickled from his nostrils and his wrist still felt like it was in a knot. By the time he got his balance, Pearce struck him with a punch to the gut, followed by an uppercut to the chin. Pivoting to the left, Pearce thrust his right heel into the thug's chest, knocking him completely off his feet.

As the masked bandit fell, the one with the gauntlets had stood up. He rushed Pearce, hands extended to grab him. Pearce charged as well, meeting the enemy halfway. As he approached within a meter, he leapt and thrust his knee forward, crashing it into the man's jaw.

Pearce landed and pressed the attack, striking the thug with two heavy strikes to the ribs. The thug moved away, dodging a third blow.

Pearce glanced over his shoulder, seeing the masked thug starting to get up. He threw a kick back, striking him in the chest and sending him back down before returning his attention to the man with the spikes. He was moving in, fists raised. He yelled as he jabbed for the loner's face, only to have his fists parried by circular blocks that caught him behind the gauntlets.

The thug grew frustrated. He took a big step toward Pearce and put all of his weight into a devastating straight punch. He felt an open hand strike up near his elbow, redirecting his fist upward. Pearce ducked under his armpit and drove an elbow into his ribs, driving two of them into his lungs.

Eyes wide with pain, the thug folded over, only to catch a strike to his temple which spun him a hundred-eighty degrees. A kick to the back of his leg dropped him to one knee. He felt Pearce reach around his head and clutch his jawline, then jerk his head sharply to the left. The last thing he felt was the snapping of his neck.

The masked bandit was back on his feet. His chest ached as he sucked in a breath. It felt as though he had been rammed by a bull. He saw his companion hit the ground, his face pointing back over his left shoulder far beyond its flexibility limits. The loner stepped away and turned to face him. He waited for the loner to grab for his gun, but he didn't, causing the thug to believe the weapons contained no bullets.

He raised his fists and gradually moved in.

Pearce waited, watching the masked man's feet. Each step came quicker until the advance turned into a run. When he was about a meter's distance, he saw one of the feet pivot, the other kicking up at him. Pearce stepped slightly to his right and blocked downward, deflecting the kick back to the ground. The thug stumbled past him, off balance. Pearce rotated left and swung a kick with his right foot, catching the enemy in the back. The thug fell forward, right into the pit.

The lizards converged on him, tearing his flesh to ribbons. The thug yelled and struggled, splashing in a pool of his own blood. Teeth ripped at his face, neck and hands, shredding his clothes and revealing new flesh.

Pearce took a breath, glanced down at his last fallen enemy as he was eaten alive, then turned to walk away.

"Mmmph!" the kid grunted again. Pearce stopped. He considered moving on. The boy grunted again. He could hear his feet scraping against the pit. Pearce turned back and stepped to the edge. The boy looked up at him. There was a slight hint of fear this time, as exhaustion was finally taking over his body.

"Do words defy you?" Pearce said, scowling. The boy grunted again. He tilted his chin up, exposing a slight red mark on his chin. Pearce kneeled for a closer look. A spider bite by the look of it. The boy was mute. "So, they do," he corrected himself.

The boy's grip on the ledge was weakening. His fingers quivered and loosened. Pearce exhaled.

None of my business, he thought. One of the hands came free. Now the boy was only holding on by one arm, which was rapidly losing its grasp. The boy looked up one last time. Now his eyes were watery. The creatures had torn the thug to shreds and he knew the same was going to happen to him.

Pearce watched the hand slip from the ledge. Finally, as if possessed by a foreign, kind-hearted spirit, he snatched him by the wrist. Relief came over the boy's face as the loner pulled him up over the ledge. He fell on his rear and scurried away from the pit, breathing rapidly for several seconds before calming down.

It was obvious to Pearce what had occurred. The boy had wandered, probably in search of camp supplies or food, and encountered the small trio of thugs. They mugged him, figured they'd throw him into the lizard pit for their own amusement, then heard Pearce coming and decided to use the boy as a distraction so they could mug him as well.

It added a small sense of satisfaction to see the lizards strip the life from the masked thug's body.

Then, as though a switch had been flipped, the boy stood to his feet. All sense of fear and terror was gone. He hustled to the thug with the broken neck and dug a few items from his pockets.

Pearce stepped behind him and pushed him to the side.

"My loot, boy. You wanted it, you should've killed 'em yourself," he said. The boy glared at him then moved in for the thug again, only to be pushed back by Pearce. He stomped his foot to the ground in protest and growled.

The loner smirked and proceeded to loot the body. The man had a cigarette lighter. He tested it, and to his surprise, it worked. He tucked it into his vest and continued, despite the boy's growling protests. Pearce suspected that the lighter had originally belonged to him. He didn't care. He continued rummaging, finding a small roll of electrical tape and nails. He kept the tape and tossed the nails.

There was something in one of the pockets that felt like a chain. Pearce pulled it out. It was a locket, shaped like a heart, with a twelve-inch chain. In the corner of his eye, he saw the boy take a step forward. A glare from the loner was enough to warn him back. Pearce opened the small locket. It was a photograph of a woman in her young twenties. At first, he thought it was a photograph that had been preserved from before the nuclear war. Then he noticed tiny details in the background: a log house, clothes that were somewhat ragged, and the image was in black and white. All cameras developed after the war were primitive in their design. This was a relatively new photograph, and it was safe to assume it didn't have sentimental value to this brutish thug.

The boy was staring at the locket in Pearce's hand. The loner felt the chain. He could find uses for it. It could serve as a component in a trap, snagging lizards and squirrels. Or he could attach a blade to the end of it and make a whip-like weapon. He noticed the boy again, his eyes never wavering.

Oh, the hell with it.

Pearce tossed it back to him. The boy gleefully caught it, a smile lighting his face. He checked the image and tucked it away.

"There. That's my last generous deed for the day," Pearce said, standing up. He waved a hand toward the boy, shooing him away. "Go away now." The boy sprinted at him. Pearce's instinctual defenses went up. His hands clenched into fists.

The boy wrapped his arms around him and hugged him.

Pearce stood frozen, his adrenaline settling. For as long as he could remember, any advancement toward him had been a hostile act. This squeezing sensation around his midsection was unfamiliar, yet somehow warm.

Pearce pushed the boy back.

"Don't know what you're doing, but that's enough."

The boy stepped back and began wandering around. He seemed aimless at first, scraping his shoes around the dirt. During this time, Pearce was checking the other dead thug that he'd choked out with the barbed chain.

The boy picked up the branch with the wire. A pebble, thrown from the loner, hit him in the cheek, shocking him and causing him to drop the stick.

"Get your own," Pearce warned. He continued looting. The boy rubbed his face and stepped away, until he saw the pack laying on the ground. Pearce heard the sound of unzipping. He whipped his head around and saw the boy peeling the pack open and pulling out his chemical set. He stood up, eyes flaring. The boy showed no concern. He grabbed the vial of disintegrating solution and tried unscrewing the cap.

"Hey!" Pearce said. "Not water. Put it down or you'll find yourself back in the pit." The boy saw the angry man's advance. He sprang to his feet, still holding the vial, then took off running. "You little prick." Pearce ran after him. The boy was like a cheetah. He passed over rocks and hills with ease, finally dropping the vial after a thousand feet or so.

Pearce quickly scooped it up. The glass was cracked but still holding together. He muttered various curse words then glanced back to the boy. He was still running, already turning into a little figure in the horizon. Pearce pondered the possibility that he belonged to another group. He was alone when he encountered the bandits. There were no other bodies nearby to hint that they had killed his guardians, and considering what he had experienced, he was in a positive emotional state.

Running like that, he would probably end up in a sandpit. Regardless, it wasn't Pearce's concern. He held the vial sideways and pointed the cracked side up to keep the solution from leaking. That electrical tape would already be put to good use.

He returned to his pack and looked down into the lizard pit. Capturing one of the creatures would be impossible now due to them having a significant food supply. He scowled. He would have to move on and find another food source before nightfall, which was rapidly approaching.

CHAPTER 6

"Where is he?" Graf said. He stared at his own shadow, which stretched four times his height to the east as the sun sank into the horizon. The thirty-two-year-old stepped away from the broken-down wagon, searching the landscape with his eyes in search of his boy, Paul. Nine years old, he was an adventurous type who showed little concern for the dangers around him. He was a product of his time, growing up having to comb the environment for food and water, at least, until a year ago when their water farm struck watery gold.

"I'm sure he's fine," Star said. Graf looked back. She was tending to the busted wagon wheel. Their two oxen bellowed as they drank their water and munched on old grain. They rested on their feet, waiting for their masters to give the signal to do their work again. It would be a while. The wheel had struck an indentation in the ground, shifting the wagon's weight suddenly. The pressure and angle caused the wheel to snap, which in turn, knocked the axle out of place.

Star tossed down a wood fragment and stood up. She looked at Graf and shook her head.

"It can't be fixed," she said. "It'll have to wait. One of us can go in the morning and get some help."

"We can't wait," Graf muttered.

"Yes, we can," Star reminded him. "We have time."

"No, we don't. He needs medical attention," Graf said. He went to the wagon and started sorting through supplies. "I'll go find him, then take one of the oxen and ride the rest of the way."

"Travel alone? Out here? At *night*?!" Star said. "It was foolish enough that we decided to cross through this place. You'd be traveling in darkness. You'll come across a band of scavengers or worse."

"We don't have time," Graf said.

"Yes, we do," Star said. "We've given him an anti-venom. It slowed down the effects, granting us time. That's why I suggested we circle around the south passage."

"The south passage? That's thirty miles out of our way. It would've doubled the time to get to the old farm."

"And *safer*," Star said. "We shouldn't have come this way."

"It was the fastest route," Graf argued. The stress was plain in his voice. He continued looking around frantically. He cupped his hands around his mouth. "PAUL!"

"Shh!" Star hissed. Long brown hair swung around her shoulders as she grabbed her brother by the shoulders. "You trying to attract every flesh-eater our way? Or scavenger?"

"I'm afraid that's what Paul might have encountered," Graf said. "So stupid of me not to keep an eye on him. He's always exploring. That's how he got bit."

"He'll be fine," Star said. "He's a smart boy. Quick-witted. He's probably on his way back right now."

Graf gently pushed her aside. Star sucked in a deep breath, stressed and frustrated, then returned to the wagon. The air was cooling rapidly. She buttoned her dusty shirt and looked for things to build a fire.

Damn, Paul had the lighter.

"Paul!" Graf called out again. Star turned, ready to scold him once more, then realized his call was a welcoming one. Paul zigzagged between the remains of half-buried vehicles as he approached their wagon. He held his locket in his hand. He was dirtier than when Graf last saw him. "Where have you been?" he said, hugging his son tight. Paul pointed behind him, then made a crawling motion with his hands. Graf understood. "You don't need to hunt for food, son. We've got some." He checked the boy's spider bite that had rendered him mute. The skin around the marks had turned dark red. Paul looked up at him and nudged his head toward the wagon. "Yes, you can go inside."

Graf watched Paul climb into the back of the wagon. He pulled out some dried pasta, a metal pan, and a canteen. He began to put water into the dish.

"Only a third of the way," Star reminded him. Paul nodded and carefully measured the water while Graf tended to the fire.

"Paul, where's the lighter?" The boy pointed back where he came. "You dropped it?" Paul shook his head then mimicked a punching motion.

Graf had not grown used to the boy's silence. Every bit of sign language the boy used was just another reminder of that fateful day when Paul had gone back around the windmill, which his family had built, exploring and studying anything he could find. There wasn't much else for a young boy to do for entertainment, especially with no friends. During his adventure, he decided to go out further and explore the dried creek. It was in a nearby bush that he discovered the spider's nest. Not understanding what it was, and oblivious to the danger, he examined it. The spider sprang and bit him on the throat.

It wasn't the venom that caused the immediate danger. The spider was carrying an infection of some kind, similar to the rumored Blood Virus. The symptoms began after a few weeks. The anti-venom they had in storage took care of the immediate threat of the venom, yet, the boy continued to get sick after a month. The bite never fully healed. His eyes began to redden. Occasionally he had days of extreme fatigue, despite spending hardly any energy.

It was when the bleeding started that Graf and Star realized something was very wrong. Realizing his boy might be fatally ill, Graf descended into a panic. His wife had abandoned them years back, which left him a wreck. He was not ready to lose his son. Paul had ups and downs, and the downs were becoming more frequent, while the ups were short lived. Right now, he was in the middle of an 'up', thanks to the medication the community doctor provided which seemed to slow the infection. Taking advantage of this, they set out to find their father in Tidal Valley.

"I don't understand?" Graf said. Paul made a walking motion and pretended to carry something over his shoulder. "A wanderer?" The boy nodded, then held up three fingers. Graf's face turned red. His boy had encountered bandits. Paul proceeded the punching motions, of which Graf wasn't entirely sure what he meant. Paul was somewhat bruised but did not look as though he had been badly beaten. Perhaps the thugs fought amongst each other. Either way, it couldn't have been good. "We can't stay," he said. "If there are bandits here…" The boy shook his head. "No bandits?" The boy nodded.

"Graf, he's safe," Star said. "That's all that matters right now. If you don't mind, I'd like to get this fire going before it gets too dark. We're gonna have to do it the old-fashioned way." She took a knife and made a groove in one of the split logs then rubbed the end of a branch against it to get a flame started.

Graf looked out one more time. The urge to chance passage through the wasteland tugged at his soul. He wanted to get his son medical attention sooner rather than later. Any delay would increase the likelihood that he would succumb to the infection. But as the sun sank lower and its gold rays turned to a dark orange and gradually to black, he knew that it would be too dangerous. Paul was fine for now and was back safe from whatever trouble he had gotten into. Graf would have to settle for that tonight.

He knelt by Star and assisted in the tedious process of starting a fire.

****

Boyle felt himself salivating as he watched the group. He was a quarter mile out, using cracked binoculars to study the three people. He wore a sleeveless shirt and brown pants and used a chain for a belt.

A companion stepped beside him.

"Should we alert Cedoz?"

"At this time of night? No. Unless you want to find yourself in a spider's funnel, Zen," Boyle said. Zen, the second-in-command of this band of the Dirt Diamond gang, nodded. Boyle returned his eyes to the binoculars. He felt a stirring down below as he studied the female. "Oh, baby, wait until you meet me," he muttered. His companion smiled, despite his apprehension.

"You wish to make the move now?"

"Good things come to those who wait," Boyle said. "There's almost no light. We'll move at dawn. Judging by the look of that wheel, they won't be going anywhere soon."

"We should probably consult with Cedoz first," Zen said. Boyle lowered the binoculars and glared at him, his blistered face expressing outrage.

"And why is that?"

"Because…" Zen tried to pick his words carefully. Cedoz was the leader of the Dirt Diamonds. His scouts were instructed to do just that; scout. He preferred to be at the front of the action and dictate the fates of those he conquered. Boyle, ten years his junior, was jealous of the authority his older brother held. He had a superiority complex, one he often displayed when in command of a scout team. And he was more quick-tempered than Cedoz, easily prone to resort to slitting the throat of anyone who challenged his rule. That razor-sharp expression was usually the first sign of that temper, and Zen now regretted bringing up the subject.

Zen cleared his throat. "I worry that Cedoz will be angered and mark your face again."

"The bastard can try," Boyle muttered. Zen felt his temper ease up as Boyle looked back to the wagon. Boyle licked his chops as though savoring a meal. "Besides, we'd have to use the flare to get his attention. There's no sense in alerting these people to our presence. We'll move in at dawn, strip the wagon for what it's worth. The girl's mine."

Zen nodded. “Then that is what we’ll do.”

“Tell the boys,” Boyle said. “Keep the fire down to embers. I don’t want to be seen.” He took one last look before the twilight darkened. He moved back and joined his men at the camp and eagerly awaited the following morning.

CHAPTER 7

Pearce woke up from a dreamless sleep, his back sore from sleeping on the granite. The sleeping bag he had taken from the bunker had spoiled him during the past few weeks. He sat up and quickly checked his solution vial. It was where he had left it, protected in a layer of black tape.

It was almost dark when he returned to the camp the previous night. He didn't find another lizard pit for almost an hour. Luckily, it took little time to catch one of the little creatures and fillet it.

He ate what little meat was left over and decided which way to continue his search. He had been traveling east nonstop for the past few days. A slight change in direction was in order. He decided to go north toward a gathering of hills. From the looks of it, there was a little more vegetation than what he had been seeing so far.

Pearce looked at the vial of dissolvent. Though it held together, he was concerned how it would endure being rattled around in the bag. He didn't want to leave the bag behind; it would be too easy to spot for anyone wandering through. However, a six-inch long vial would not attract attention. Still, he wanted it properly hidden. He checked around, then dug at a hollow spot in the gulley, placed the vial in the hole, then gently buried it. He placed a Y-shaped branch close by. To anyone walking by, it would mean nothing. For him, however, it served as a marker to where he hid the item.

Satisfied, he continued northeast.

****

The first couple of hours brought the same results as before. The land was barren, with no sign of any vegetation, much less a rare Red Flower. Pearce remained patient until his coughing acted up. The reminder of his impending doom brought frustration, as well as a sense of doubt. Perhaps this was all a wild goose chase.

Despite those doubts, the will to survive drove him forward. He moved patiently, reminding himself he'd rather fight for every last moment of life than sit around waiting for the inevitable.

He found a small patch of trees and decided to check near there. Aside from a few weeds, there was no flower of any kind. He then moved eastward past a few rolling hills. There were more of those poisonous red dandelions that deceived his vision at first glance.

Never before had he experienced such hate for a simple plant. Each time he saw the red dandelion, his mind toyed with him, thinking he had discovered his goal. He continued east, finding the ruins of what had been a hospital and the parking lot that surrounded it. The concrete had been withered to dust, the vehicles in pieces. Some had human skeletons that stared endlessly through the shattered windshields, their jaws agape as though screaming in horror.

Pearce slowly moved between the ruined cars and trucks, his hand resting on his revolver. This would be an easy place for someone to hide. He didn't smell any human stench in the air, nor did he hear any movement. He kept going, noticing a small bush that had sprouted near the building structure. Quickening his pace, he weaved between the obstacles until he reached the destination.

He dug his heels into the ground, stopping himself.

Murky green leaves swayed over leathery tentacle vines that extended from the bulb-shaped head of the Sapper. Pearce's hand moved from his revolver to his knife. Bullets would do little against this mutant, flesh-eating plant. He slowly stepped back, carefully watching one of the vines that rested inches from his foot. Like a sleeping giant, the leathery bulb pulsed as it waited.

Like the tentacles of a kraken, those vines would snag unsuspecting prey and drag them to the beast. That bulb would peel open like flower petals, exposing a gigantic mouth that would engulf the meal, then seal it in before dissolving it in a sappy acidic substance that digested the victim alive.

After distancing himself several feet, he quickened his pace, putting several more yards between him and the Sapper.

Damn wasteland, he thought. He altered course, going west this time, moving along the rolling hills. He found a paved road that remained somewhat intact and followed it. Soon, the hospital was out of sight behind him.

After another hour, he found a semi-truck tire lying in the dirt. He sat on it and removed his boots, shaking out the dust that accumulated before placing them back on. After finishing, he allowed himself to rest for a minute. He took a drink from his canteen, then stared out into the surrounding landscape. Directly ahead was nothing but scorched, dry earth. To his right, he could see the beach-colored soil that made up a couple of sandpits. They were spaced about a hundred feet apart from each other, each surrounded by a few rocks and discarded skeletons from unfortunate prey. To his left was a small hill, containing a single withering tree. Close by it was a patch of grass that had turned grey. It was wilted due to lack of water.

Everything was dying here.

Pearce put it out of his mind and sipped more water.

There was a tickling against his leg. Pearce swallowed, feeling something scraping against his hamstring. He sprang off the tire and turned around, his hand ready to draw his sidearm.

Frolicking legs extended from the middle of the tire as a two-foot long tarantula pulled itself free. Black fangs extended from its mouth, having narrowly missed its mark. Pearce drew his knife as the arachnid pulled itself from under the tire. It advanced, those expressionless black eyes fixed on him. The fangs twitched, ready to sting him and render him paralyzed so his blood could be gradually drawn from his body, then used as a vessel for it to lay its eggs.

It wasted no time darting at him. Pearce backpedaled and held his knife down, ready to plunge it into the creature's head.

Before he could make his move, the creature leapt, its eight legs acting like springs launching simultaneously. Pearce ducked and rolled to his left, the spider passing directly over him. It splashed down into the dirt, rolling onto its back. Its legs flailed, then hyperextended to one side, rolling it back to its correct position.

Pearce rolled to his feet and faced the creature. It was already darting toward him again. He backtracked, prepping his knife for the creature's next leap. He understood its method of attack now; it was just a matter of timing.

It sprang again, ascending six feet into the air. Fangs protruded, trailing lemon-colored venom.

Pearce sidestepped and slashed downward, severing three of the four legs on the spider's left side. It hit the ground and thrashed, spilling blood from its three stumps. The loner moved in and pressed his foot down on it, pinning the spider to the ground, then plunged his blade through its head and twisted. The spider convulsed then curled its remaining legs as it took its eternal deathly pose.

Pearce stepped back and sheathed his knife, while staring at the dead arachnid. This wasteland never offered a break. It was a haunting reminder that death lurked literally *everywhere* in these parts.

His frustration was rising again. For weeks he had searched for the Red Flower, only to be attacked by carnivorous lizards, jumped by bandits, stumble into poisonous and carnivorous plants, and now nearly stung by a tarantula.

He kicked its frizzed corpse, sending it rolling back toward the sandpits. It bounced over a rock, stirring something behind it before settling several feet away. Pearce saw the tip of vegetation swaying behind the rock, its peace disturbed by the tumbling spider. Pearce approached, cautious, as the plant was directly on the edge of an eight-foot wide sandpit.

As he neared, he spotted a round green leaf. It was not a patch of weeds or a bush. He caught a glimpse of red.

Probably another damn dandelion.

Yet, there didn't appear to be any thorns. Pearce came within two meters of the rock. He had his rifle unstrung at this point and aimed prudently at the pit. Stepping over a broken ribcage, he took a closer look at the plant.

He blinked repeatedly, making sure his eyes did not deceive him. They did not. He had found what he was looking for. The Red Flower was here!

Pearce breathed a sigh of relief. There was a triumphant feeling in his chest. After what seemed like endless searching, he had completed his goal. The inner struggle of finding the flower was gone. It was there, in perfect health, a few dry bones laying beside it.

Then came the realization of the scenario; he had to dig it out.

Pearce watched the pit as he tried to devise a plan. It didn't take long for him to realize that he didn't have many options. The plant was there, and until he was ready to create the lifesaving potion from its petals, he would have to preserve the plant and keep it alive. Such a procedure was more delicate than simply grabbing it by the stem and tearing it free, then running off. He would have to dig it out by the roots.

Pearce inched his way closer. He now had his rifle shouldered, his finger resting on the trigger. The sandpit rested undisturbed. The bones indicated that the nest was not abandoned.

He picked up a rock, then tossed it near the nest, making sure it thumped audibly. He gripped his weapon and waited for the creature to emerge. It didn't. The sandpit was as still as ice.

Pearce rolled another rock near it, only to produce the same result. Finally, he picked up a larger rock and tossed it directly into the sandpit.

Sand splashed in little waves as the pit absorbed the rock. It was out of sight in an instant. Pearce aimed the muzzle.

Still nothing! Either the creature was asleep, had moved on, or had recently fed. Considering the number of skeletons, that wasn't unlikely. Pearce gazed at the flower. It was so close, yet so far. He could feel beads of sweat spilling down his back, soaking his shirt.

It was as though the wasteland was making fun of him. The gift of life rested right there, on the edge of death.

It was clear he would not be able to draw it out and shoot it. He watched the flower lean in the breeze, his eyes thirsting for the medicine in those red petals. He didn't trek this far for nothing. He placed his pack down and dug out a gardening rake. One of the tips had been broken, and the handle was severely cracked. It didn't matter. He needed the tool for this one purpose.

He let his rifle hang by the strap as he approached the flower. He held the rake in one hand and his knife in the other. Each step was taken slowly and silently. It was almost ten minutes before he crossed the ten feet of distance.

Pearce knelt by the flower. He glanced once more at the pit. Seeing no movement, he carefully begun work on extracting the flower. He raked the knife in a circular motion, weakening the soil, then ran the tip of his knife into the ground. He kept the incisions six inches from where the stem entered the ground, making sure to provide plenty of root for it to survive.

His palms grew sweaty as he gradually dug a few inches deeper. He tilted his blade, cutting directly under the plant. When he was done, he extracted a small, cone-shaped piece of soil from the earth, the flower protruding from the top of it. He looked at the prize. It was healthy, hydrated, and waiting to be used. Pearce felt victorious, even feeling a smile about to crease his face.

The sandpit erupted. Soil spewed in all directions, making way for two enormous grey pincers.

Pearce fell backward, dropping the flower as the claws lunged in his direction. They snapped shut inches from his chest, then retracted to pull the arachnid's body from the pit.

Mandibles flailed over a huge pincer mouth as the scorpion emerged from its pit. Twelve eyes locked their gaze onto the human. Like a homing missile, it moved in on him, propelled by eight enormous legs.

It was a little one, only eight feet in length, not counting its coiled tail. Nonetheless, it was as deadly as they came, carrying more than enough venom to put him into cardiac arrest. Not that it needed to. Those claws were more than capable of ripping him apart in seconds.

It hissed ferociously, both hungry and agitated. Pearce kicked his feet, pushing himself back as he grabbed for his rifle. He saw the tail quivering as it cocked back. The creature moved in.

Pearce dug his heels into the ground and launched himself back. The tail vaulted, the stinger stabbing down between his knees. Pearce scuttled back on all fours, putting another meter between him and the creature. Sitting up, he shouldered his rifle and fired half his magazine into the creature.

The first ten bullets hit its shell and bounced off, the next five managing to breach near the left shoulder. Feeling no pain, the scorpion advanced. Pearce scuttled back, using one hand to push himself up. The claws clanked together then reached at him again.

He jumped back, feeling the tips grazing his vest. The creature didn't stop. It lashed its tail again, forcing the loner to dive to his right to avoid it. He rolled up to one knee, turned back, then fired again. The gun rattled until all fifteen remaining bullets punched their way into the creature's hide. Some ricocheted while others successfully breached near the leg joints. Yellow blood spilled onto the dirt.

Muttering curses, Pearce ejected the mag and reloaded.

The scorpion corrected its path and moved at him again. Its tail coiled, ready for another strike. Pearce continued backtracking, keeping just out of reach. Then, with a tremendous *thud*, he struck something hard. He glanced back. A huge boulder had blocked his path, keeping him from retreating.

"Shit."

The creature sprawled its arms out. The tail lifted over its head.

Pearce aimed high and released a bullet spray. The stinger burst into small fragments, spilling venom over the scorpion's back. The tail retracted, its stinger dangling by a loose piece of flesh and shell.

Pearce continued firing into the creature's face as it came at him. He shrieked as the pincers closed around his waist. They lifted him off the ground and pulled him toward the clicking mandibles. He squeezed the trigger again.

Click.

The magazine was empty.

He felt the pincers begin to tighten. With a little effort, they would slice him in half as though he were butter.

Pearce dropped the weapon and drew his revolver.

The jaws opened.

He thrust his arm out, driving the weapon into its throat, then squeezed the trigger. The creature shuddered, its claws releasing their grip. With the gun still in its mouth, Pearce fired again. The scorpion lurched back, blood and saliva spewing from its mandibles. It thrashed in a horrific display before rolling on its back. Its legs and tail thrashed like a horseshoe crab turned upside down, then slowed into twitching motions. It spasmed one final time, arching its back, then curled into a deathly pose.

Pearce backed away and reloaded his assault rifle. He checked his waist where he was grabbed. Aside from a couple of abrasions in his vest, there were no cuts or broken bones. Had it squeezed just a little tighter, the results would've been much different.

He watched the creature for a full minute to make sure it was dead. He opened his revolver cylinder and removed the two empty cartridges. After tossing them aside, he reached into his pocket and pulled two of his three loose rounds and inserted them into the empty slots. He holstered the revolver and hurried back to the sandpit.

The flower was partly buried under a layer of sand from the scorpion's emergence. He dusted it off and held it up. The roots had lost some of their soil, but other than that, the flower appeared in healthy condition. Pearce carried it to his pack and dug out a glass jar, tucked inside a layer of foam protection. He inserted the plant into the jar, then added some water from his canteen. The roots were fast to begin absorbing the moisture. The plant was close to withering. He suspected it had only lasted this long due to feeding off blood that had spilled from the scorpion's previous meals.

The loner packed the flower away. There was one last thing to do: return to the camp and retrieve the vial. Then it would be time to generate the medicine that was said to cure all illnesses. Those red petals meant life. And life was all Pearce desired.

CHAPTER 8

Graf woke up to deafening gunshots, followed by the deep bellows of the oxen. He sprang out of the wagon, only to be struck in the face by something hard. The world seemed to spin as he collapsed to his hands and knees. A kick to the ribs rolled him onto his back.

There were eight people, all dressed in dusty black or brown clothing. Seven of them were men, the other a woman. She had shaggy black hair and wore a thin leather vest that barely concealed her breasts.

Then he saw Star. She was lunging at one of the men, successfully plowing a fist into his groin. As Graf's vision cleared, he realized that the men were ganging up around her. Their intent was obvious.

"Don't even think about it, you—"

The female bandit plowed the toe of her boot into his gut, blowing his air out and rolling him back down. Graf gasped for air. He looked back to the gang. Any hope of resistance came to an end when he saw the firearms they carried. Three of the men had rifles, two carried pistols, and one other had a shotgun, while the female carried a revolver on each hip. In addition, they each held a sharp or blunt instrument of some kind. This band of thieves was well-armed.

One of the thugs barked at those who crowded Star.

"Not so fast," he said, pointing to one who was about to unfasten his belt. "You know the rules." The thug zipped back up and backed away. It was enough for Graf to deduce that this one with the chain-linked belt was the leader. He leaned in close to Star and grazed a finger along her bare shoulder. What started as a caress quickly turned into a tight grab. He started tugging at her, attempting to drag her toward the back of the wagon, while one hand worked on unfastening his pants.

Star screamed and threw a kick between his legs. The thug yelled and doubled over. He quickly righted himself and shoved her back against the wagon. He whipped the pistol over her face, knocking her to the ground.

"Hey!" Graf moaned. The pistol was now aimed at him. Graf froze. He remained on his hands and knees, quivering in pain. The leader turned back toward his sister. His teeth were clenched, both from pain and anger. He snarled and kicked Star in the stomach, driving her into the busted wagon wheel.

The oxen bellowed again. They were both on the ground, bleeding from gunshots to their necks. Their noises seemed to aggravate the leader further. He stomped up to the front of the wagon and aimed at them.

Graf looked away and closed his eyes, shuddering with each gunshot, which was followed by a high-pitched squeal from the dying animals.

Boyle seethed as he watched the life fade from the oxen. Blood spurted from their bullet wounds as they twitched and spasmed. Breathing heavily, he looked over at his companions, all of whom watched him nervously. He straightened himself out, then twirled his pistol like a cowboy, marveling at the two oxen he had shot to death.

"Plenty of meat for breakfast, lunch, and dinner, boys!" he announced. Zen stood by the wagon. He refused to respond, as the only thing he could think of was Cedoz. He probably would have wanted the oxen alive. Not only that, but Boyle had wasted precious bullets on them. He looked over at Graf and tipped the muzzle of his shotgun toward the thugs standing near him.

"Search him!"

The female thug, along with one of the men, dug at Graf's clothing. They pulled his jacket off and tossed it aside. They dug in his pockets and pulled his belongings out.

"Should we kill them?" one of them asked.

"Not this one," Boyle said, looking at Star. "Search the wagon! And tie her up!" He put his foot on Star's shoulder. She was conscious, her left brow red from the blow. There was a small cut near her hairline that bled down near her eye. Boyle stared at her exposed midsection and thought of his lustful ambition. All it did, however, was remind him of the aching pain down there.

He stepped back and allowed his men to put rope around her ankles. He would have his way when he was good and ready. As for the man, he had no use for him. Boyle looked at his pistol then at Graf, who was watching the ransacking of his wagon.

Boyle noticed a nervousness in his eyes that wasn't there a few moments ago. Graf was watching the wagon, unblinkingly. Boyle and Zen shared a glance.

It suddenly hit Boyle: there was something specific in that wagon that he didn't want found. He stepped up to Graf and grabbed him by his hair.

Graf gritted his teeth and looked his captor in the eyes.

"What's on your mind?" Boyle asked. Graf said nothing. Boyle tightened his grip. "Let me re-phrase: what's in there that you don't want us to find?"

"Nothing," Graf said. His eyes went back to the wagon. He didn't see Paul in there. Perhaps he wandered off before the bandits arrived. All he could do right now was hope his son found a good place to hide.

The four bandits ripped through the wagon. They quickly ate into some of the food and water, while tossing spare clothes out onto the dirt. They ripped the tarp, exposing the interior to Boyle.

"Look at all of this water!" one of them said.

"Food too! Packaged and nicely preserved," another said.

"There's a grand supply in this wagon alone. These people have a nice settlement somewhere," Zen said. The bandits ripped the tarp away, exposing the skeletal structure of the wagon and all the contents within.

Now, there was relief in Graf's eyes. Paul was not in there. Boyle noticed this. He pulled Graf's face close to his.

"There's someone else in your camp, isn't there?!" he growled. Graf pulled back, turning his face away from the bandit's blistered face. The female bandit knelt by him, her smile as sadistic as Boyle's. He saw her draw a knife from her boot and felt its tip press threateningly against his back.

"There's nothing to tell," he groaned. Boyle snickered. He turned to his men.

"Search around! There's one more!" he ordered. The bandits disembarked and branched out. They checked around a few nearby rocks, finding nothing, and branched out further.

Star struggled to escape from her binds.

"Just take what you want and leave," she said.

"Believe me, I will," Boyle said. The aching was finally subsiding. He sneered at her as he approached. "I'm gonna take *everything*. First, you will tell me where the third member of your party is."

"There is no third member," she lied. Boyle chuckled again. Neither of them was good at lying. It was a drawback of being brought up with good morals in a lawless land.

"Where'd this water come from?" Boyle asked.

"We found a river," Graf lied.

"Okay, now the lying's getting on my nerves! There are no rivers for a hundred miles," Boyle said. "And I know the old man with the water farm didn't harvest any! So, tell me where you found it, and I might consider only having her *once*." Boyle glanced down at Star and smiled.

Graf gulped. He knew this gang would slaughter the people back at his camp. It would be a massacre. The natural thing to do was to lie. The problem was: Boyle would see right through it and unleash hell on Star until he got the truth. And even then, he would probably continue.

"Maybe the third member of your party might be persuaded to say something," Boyle continued. "We'll find him… or her, whichever." He waited. "No answer? Alright, then."

Star screamed and kicked as Boyle put his hands on her. She writhed, unable to fight through her binds. Boyle laughed sadistically as his hands went to her waistline.

"Tell me what I want to know, and I'll stop—eh, who am I kidding? I'm as bad of a liar as you!" Boyle laughed. Star screamed as he pulled at her clothes.

Graf pushed himself off the ground. "Get your hands off—AGH!" he yelled as the female hammered the knife handle to his head. He fell forward, his vision hazy. Through the haze he saw his sister twisting on the ground, struggling against the bandit leader.

Suddenly, there was movement from under the wagon.

Paul let himself drop from the rafters that lined the belly of the wagon where he had suspended himself out of view. Boyle looked up from his victim just in time to see the boy emerge, rock in hand. He tossed that rock like a softball, planting it squarely between Boyle's eyes.

The bandit's head snapped back as he fell off Star. He rolled back, face bloodied by the time he hit the ground.

"Paul! RUN!" Graf and Star yelled at once. Paul hesitated. He had come out of hiding after seeing what these evil people were about to do to his father and aunt.

The bandit woman approached with the knife.

"Run!" Graf repeated.

Paul darted to his right, passing between the two thugs that guarded his father. They reached for him but missed due to his incredible speed.

Boyle sat up, his faced lined with streaks of red.

"Get that little twerp!" he shouted.

Zen and the female took off after Paul, while the rest of the gang regrouped by the wagon. Boyle tried to get up, but in his dizziness, fell back to the ground. Two of his men tried helping him up.

"I'm fine! I'm fine!" he growled, then pointed at their captives. "Tie him up and put him with her. Once Zen gets back with their boy, we'll find out where they've been getting their water."

Graf tensed. His eyes welled at the thought of these horrible creatures torturing his child. He looked back over his shoulder. Paul had already made considerable distance. He was heading west where he had explored the previous evening.

Please Paul, get away.

Zen grunted as he pushed himself to his limits. The boy was fast, maintaining at least a few hundred feet of distance. The female bandit was closer, possibly fifty feet ahead. She was visibly frustrated. It was clear from the get-go that the boy was easily outrunning them.

She yanked one of her revolvers free and aimed it.

"Hold up!" Zen ordered. Either she didn't hear him or was ignoring him. Regardless, the woman's aim didn't waiver. She squeezed the trigger then looked to see if she hit the target.

Paul was still running, unfazed. She missed him.

"Damn!" she hissed.

Paul ducked his head when he heard the gunshot. The bullet whistled as it whizzed by his head. He summoned all his energy, pushing himself as fast as he could go.

He looked up and opened his mouth to scream, only to have a dull moan escape. He was on the verge of running straight into a large sandpit. He threw himself to the side and ran around the edge, then immediately made a few feet of distance.

Paul continued west, feeling his body already starting to ache. His illness was acting up. He knew he couldn't run forever, and it was clear that these bandits would not stop.

He needed to find help.

In this wasteland, there was only one person to turn to.

CHAPTER 9

Pearce located his camp and knelt by the marker he had set up. He dug at the loose soil until he uncovered the vial. It was safe, undamaged from the burial, and ready to be put to good use.

He opened his pack and dug out the processer and the Red Flower. It was small, about as big as a dandelion. It was only enough to create a single dose of antibiotic. He removed the petals and crushed them down in a small ceramic bowl, then stirred the pieces, oozing the sap within. He placed the residue into a glass container, then added the dissolvent, which liquefied the proteins, allowing them to be injected.

The processer stirred like a blender, mixing the flower into a thin red liquid. It was complete after a few short rotations. Pearce removed the container and emptied the contents into the syringe. It was ready for injection. The moment of truth was here. He tapped his left arm to expose a vein.

Gunshots echoed overhead.

Pearce grabbed for his rifle and looked around. It was coming from somewhere to the east. He couldn't see from where he was at. After several seconds, he could hear running feet.

The injection would have to wait. He placed the cap back on the syringe and covered it in protective foam. He got to his feet and stepped out of the gulley. The sounds of running were still distant, though drawing closer. He moved further out, cautiously watching the horizon.

Breathing heavily and covered in sweat, Paul stopped near the lizard pit and looked around. The mysterious man was nowhere to be found. He looked back. The bandits were closing in, and judging on how trigger happy the female was, they were eager to do harm.

He continued past the lizard pit and moved southeast.

"Get back here!" Zen yelled, frustrated. The boy darted from view, weaving between a few twisting rock structures. The two bandits branched out to increase their vantage point.

"I see him!" The female pointed. She fired another shot, missing again. Angered, she continued to run after the boy, while Zen circled to the left.

Paul wheezed. His lungs burned, as did his muscles. He started to cough, which made breathing increasingly difficult. That horrible infection was spreading its evil through his veins.

He leaned forward and coughed, while still trying to run. It felt as though an invisible hand was squeezing his lungs. Paul's run slowed into a stumble. The coughing intensified. He could hear his pursuers closing in behind him. He pushed himself into another run, only to stumble again after a few hundred feet. Dazed and exhausted, he fell to his hands and knees.

After sucking in a deep breath, he looked up.

He saw a man standing ahead of him, his tactical gear contrasting against the grey background of the wasteland. It was him! He had found the loner.

Pearce raised his weapon as another shot cracked the air. The sounds of running feet drew nearer. Then the runner came into view. He fell to his knees, coughed, then looked up at him.

It was that same boy!

"Not you again," Pearce muttered.

He saw two people rapidly approaching. One man and one woman. They both had firearms.

The female thug drew her other revolver the moment she saw the wanderer. She would not bother asking questions. She saw all the gear he wore and wanted it for herself.

Pearce already had his rifle aimed. He squeezed the trigger as soon as those revolvers started pointing his way. A three round burst struck the woman across the chest, ravaging her lungs and heart. The force of the shots knocked her back, causing her arms to whip upward, discharging both guns into the air.

He saw the man with the shotgun closing in. Zen's expression turned to one of anger and vengeance. He fired the shotgun, missing Pearce as he dove forward. The loner kept going, avoiding another spread-shot blast that peppered the ground behind him.

Pearce somersaulted and came up to one knee. He turned and returned fire with a three-round burst. One of the bullets caught Zen in the upper left shoulder, causing him to jolt. He did a complete 360-degree turn and fired a blind shot at the loner as he completed the spin. The shot struck one of the twisted rock structures, exploding a fraction of it into dust, which blew over Pearce's eyes, momentarily blinding him. Pearce ducked behind cover, avoiding another shotgun blast from Zen. He waited for a moment, cleared his vision, and prepared to make his final assault.

He knew the shotgun that the man carried. It only held five shells at a time. He just needed to make him waste one more, then he could finish him off with a knife instead of using up another bullet.

Zen advanced, his bullet wound leaking blood into his shirt. He pressed the shotgun to his other shoulder and waited for the loner to peek from behind cover.

"Come on. Come on," he snarled. He grabbed the boy by the back of his shirt. Paul struggled until the man's arm was wrapped around his neck.

Pearce peeked, seeing the thug holding the boy as a human shield.

"I'll kill him," Zen threatened.

"Okay. I'm waiting," Pearce said, his voice monotone. Zen clenched his teeth.

"I WILL," he continued, pressing the shotgun to Paul's back.

"I know. You said that already," Pearce said. *Go ahead and waste your last shell,* his mind finished. He watched around the edge of the rock. The thug was breathing rapidly, growing more nervous by the second. Realizing the hostage threat was getting him nowhere, he positioned the shotgun over the boy's shoulder.

Paul relaxed himself and waited. Several quiet seconds passed, each one feeling like an hour. During this time, he felt Zen's hold on him slightly loosen. Finally, he kicked a leg back into his groin, shuddering Zen's body, while thrusting his arms up into the shotgun. The bandit fired instinctually, his blast trailing uselessly into the air.

Pearce heard the shot and sprang from cover, slinging his rifle in favor of his knife. The thug snarled angrily and threw the boy to the ground. He reached into his pocket, frantically trying to find more shells for his weapon.

Zen's eyes locked on the loner and saw that he held a knife.

Cocky bastard wants to fight like a man! he thought. Zen gripped his shotgun like a club, raised it high over his shoulder, and advanced. He had a smile on his face as he closed in within ten feet.

Pearce threw the knife.

That smile disappeared as the blade plunged into his neck. Zen staggered, his eyes and mouth wide. He fell to his knees and dropped his shotgun. He kept this frozen pose as the life slipped from him, concluding with him slowly sinking backward.

Paul quickly got up onto his feet, calming himself. The loner extracted his knife and wiped the blood off its blade using the thug's pantleg.

"This is the *second* time I saved your a—" The boy hugged Pearce. For the *second* time, he was caught off guard by this action. He pushed Paul away and, without wasting any more words, he inspected the bodies. There were seven shells in Zen's pocket. He took them and loaded them into the shotgun before moving on to the female. Her revolvers carried .38 caliber rounds, which could be fired from his .357. Though this clash involved gunfire, it at least resulted in a decent loot.

Paul stepped up to him and started pointing toward the west. Pearce followed his finger, looked in the direction he pointed, then shook his head.

"No. You're alive. That's all the favors you're getting from me," he said. Paul grabbed his arm and pulled. Pearce didn't budge an inch as he finished collecting the bullets from the dead woman. The boy seemed desperate for his attention. "Here…" Pearce took one of the revolvers and shoved it into his hands, "take that and learn to use it. All the trouble you've been getting into, might not be a bad idea." He gave a quick demonstration of how to open the cylinder. The gun was empty, of course. Pearce was never in the habit of giving another person a loaded weapon, which could be turned on him in an instant.

Paul backed up, feeling increasingly desperate. He did not know how to communicate to the loner about his family's situation. And even if he did, it wasn't clear if the loner would even help.

Paul glanced around, remembering that the loner carried a pack that he valued. It was not here. If Pearce was without it, it had to be close by. Paul quickly moved toward the gulley while Pearce finished up his loot. Paul found the gulley and saw the pack.

He hesitated before picking it up, recalling how harshly the loner reacted to him going through it the previous day. However, it was the only way to lure him to the wagon. He breathed and relaxed himself, then picked up the bag.

Pearce pocketed a watch and a box of matches in addition to a small container of gunpowder. This loot was getting better and better. He was about to step away when he noticed something on the woman's hand. At first, it appeared to be a scar, jet black in color. Then Pearce noticed the diamond shape. It was a tattoo.

The other thug had it too, on the same hand. Pearce double-checked his supplies and stood up. It was the symbol of the Dirt Diamonds, one of the most ruthless gangs in the wasteland. Word had gotten around that they had raped and pillaged whole communities like ancient Vikings. From what he understood, there were close to a hundred members in this gang. They carried an arsenal of firearms and explosives.

If they were in the area, they would eventually find these bodies. Pearce knew the reputation of the leader, Cedoz. Once the bodies were discovered, a massive manhunt would begin, and would not stop until the perpetrator was found. If the perpetrator could not be identified, Cedoz would even massacre nearby settlements to increase the likelihood that he had his revenge. Out here in this wasteland, there wouldn't be much to absolve Pearce. The gang would probably slaughter him anyway, the only difference now would be there would soon be a manhunt.

He would have to move quick and escape the area.

"You little twerp," he muttered. "You realize what you did, you—" his voice trailed off as he saw Paul several hundred feet out. He held his pack in one hand, materials inside…including his syringe! Pearce leapt to his feet. The boy took off running to the east. Pearce growled various curses as he ran after him. He had no choice: He could not leave without what he came here for.

You little shit! I should've let the lizards strip your flesh!

CHAPTER 10

"I'm gonna kill that boy," Boyle said, taunting Graf. He paced back and forth, his face still caked in his own blood. His forehead throbbed, especially in the notch between his eyes where the rock had struck him. He continuously glanced to the west, waiting for Zen to return with the prize.

Graf and Star were both tied to the side of the wagon, the latter piercing through the bandit leader with her gaze. She wanted to kill him desperately, especially if he dared to attempt again to set himself on her. There were five men standing nearby, three of them holding rifles. The fourth had a handgun, which appeared to be well-maintained. She and Graf had both learned to shoot, and had occasion to defend themselves in the past, though the only bandits were usually small duos or trios. Not larger groups like this one.

"I see someone!" one of the bandits shouted. All eyes looked to the west. Boyle squinted. The boy was barely recognizable in the distance. He almost looked like a grey dot.

"It's the boy," he said.

"There's someone behind him," another thug said. "Is it Zen?"

"I don't see Aria," said another. The bandits murmured in agreement. Their female companion was nowhere in sight.

"That must be Zen," Boyle said. "He chased the little bastard out there and BACK!" The group chuckled. Boyle pointed to two of his men. "Go out there and help the idiot. Don't shoot the boy. That'll be *my* pleasure."

Graf strained against his restraints, much to the pleasure of Boyle. The two men ran out, cackling to themselves as they closed in on the boy. They could even hear the man whom they thought was Zen yelling at the boy as he chased him toward the wagon.

****

"I swear to Christ if you don't stop, I'm gonna twist your little head off and toss you in the pit," Pearce snarled, weaving around a large sandpit as he chased the boy. He was less than fifty feet ahead of him now. The boy was fast, even when visibly fatigued. Pearce could tell he was beginning to falter. The heavy breathing was evident, as well as the spitting and clutching of his stomach.

Paul could see the wagon ahead, despite his vision starting to blur. His hair glistened with his sweat. His clothes felt increasingly heavy as he went on. His stomach felt like it was about to implode.

Pearce raced toward the slowing kid. By the time he caught up, Paul had stopped entirely. Pearce grabbed the pack off of his back.

"Boy, I can understand why so many people are trying to kill you. You seem to have a knack for pissing people off!"

The boy didn't respond. Instead, he pointed directly ahead. At the same time, Pearce could hear approaching footsteps and banter. He looked ahead, seeing two more armed men with automatic rifles rapidly approaching. His eyes went from the guns to their hands.

They both wore the Dirt Diamond symbol.

"Oh, shit," he muttered.

The bandits wore smiles, thinking Zen had caught the boy. Those smiles faded when they realized that he was not in fact, Zen, but was holding Zen's shotgun.

Pearce already had that shotgun pointed. Tilting it toward the one on the right, he fired high. The pellets hit in a tight grouping, caving the bandit's face inward. Pearce pumped the weapon and fired at the other, hitting him square in the chest. The bandit reeled backward, his rifle discharging a few rounds into the air.

The boy got on his feet and moved forward. He pointed to the wagon. Pearce saw the wagon and three bandits that were now moving rapidly toward the sound of gunfire.

"Great. Just great," he said. It appeared it was just a small group of five. He had moments to kill them before they alerted the rest of the gang. There was no choice; he had to engage. He switched from the shotgun to the rifle, then glanced at the boy.

Paul had deliberately used him, probably to save himself and the two people tied to the wagon. Had a full-grown man pulled this stunt, Pearce would've killed him. The thought even ran through his mind, though something in him prevented that.

"Here," he said, tossing the shotgun. Paul caught it, looked it over, then glanced back at the loner. Pearce realized he didn't quite understand how to use it. The bandits were closing in. Three hundred yards now. He rushed over to Paul and helped him grip the weapon properly. "Up against your shoulder like this. Line your eyes along these iron sights here. Squeeze the trigger. Pump this thing back, which'll eject the empty shell, then shoot again."

Paul held the weapon properly and nodded. Pearce stepped away, then looked back once more.

"You have three shots. Oh…and if you shoot me, I'll be sure to take your head off before I die."

He hated himself for this. Never before had he even considered giving a loaded weapon to another person, much less a kid. It was part of the rule of survival when traveling alone; always be in control of the weapons, and never trust anyone.

Pearce pulled back the cocking lever on his assault rifle, then charged the four bandits.

Boyle had ordered the men to engage when he had heard the gunshots. They were quick to advance, while he waited behind with the captives.

The men ran quickly, then slowed when they realized the stranger was charging them. They started to branch out. However, they barely took tactical formation when the stranger opened fire.

This group was overconfident, traveling so close to one another. It made aiming especially easy. Pearce opened fire, striking one of the bandits directly in the chest.

His torso opened up as though an invisible chainsaw was tearing into it. Blood and tissue splattered as he faceplanted dead onto the ground.

Pearce continued firing, striking another in the leg. The bandit yelped then dove out of the way, avoiding additional shots. He got to his feet and ran, blindly returning fire. He ran toward the boy, intending to use him as a human shield. He reached out to grab him.

"You're coming with—" the bandit froze, seeing Zen's shotgun in the boy's hands.

Paul positioned the weapon like the loner showed him, then squeezed the trigger. The recoil instantly sent him backward. The shot struck the bandit square in the center, launching him a few inches off his feet before barreling him on the dirt. He settled on his back, lifeless eyes in a permanent state of shock. His chest was blown wide open as though hit with an explosive.

Pearce ran to his left, avoiding a few rounds sent his way from the third Dirt Diamond. He fired a few rounds back but missed. The bandit was moving in frantic motions, unsure if he wanted to stand and fight or retreat. After several tense moments, the shots stopped. He saw the bandit stop and try to reload his pistol.

Pearce took the opportunity to steady his aim. He put his eye along the sight and fired a single round.

Blood splattered from the bandit's arm, causing the weapon to fall from his hands. He stumbled back, fell to his knees, then righted himself again. Pearce had fired slightly wide to the right, though he at least was successful in disarming the enemy.

The Dirt Diamond saw the loner approach. Finally, all loyalty to his gang had become secondary to his own survival. He retreated into the wasteland, ignoring the gaping hole in his shoulder as he distanced himself from the warrior. He looked back to gauge the distance. The man wasn't pursuing. The bandit turned his head forward. He screamed and dug his heels into the earth to keep himself from falling into the sandpit directly ahead. He twisted and fell to his knees, his toes resting over the edge. His boots were partly buried in the loose sand, indicating how close he had come to falling in.

There was a brief sigh of relief before he started crawling away.

The sand exploded as the huge scorpion burst from its lair. In one swift movement, it hauled its eighteen-foot body length out of the pit and snatched the Dirt Diamond with its pincers. The man struggled as razor claws sliced into his midsection.

The tail vaulted, punching the stinger between his shoulder blades. The venom proved useless, as the barb came out through his chest. The thug slumped dead in its claws as it sank back into its pit. The sand swirled then settled, obscuring the grotesque sound of munching.

Pearce reloaded his weapon and rushed toward the wagon. There was only one thug left to kill.

Boyle gulped as he watched his men be taken down one by one. His pistol shook in his hand as he watched the stranger advancing toward him. He aimed and fired, missing by a mile, then fired again. Finally, he turned and ran back to the hostages. He grabbed Star and unhooked her from the wagon.

She knew he intended to use her as a human shield. His movements were frantic and uncoordinated. He had to tug on the binds at least three times before he freed her from the wagon.

Star seized the opportunity and kneed him in the groin. It served two purposes: It was vulnerable, and it brought her personal satisfaction. Boyle lurched back, losing his hold on her. He whipped the pistol again, grazing her on the chin. It wasn't a solid impact but enough to drive her back.

Boyle snarled; he'd had enough. He pointed his pistol to shoot her.

A shot rang out. Blood splattered from Boyle's abdomen. The thug spun and fell to his hands and knees, dropping the pistol. He retched as he frantically crawled away. He looked back, seeing the shooter coming within a hundred feet.

There was only one thing to do. Boyle knew he would die, and there was no way he would be able to seek revenge personally on these people. The fact that his group had wronged them first had no bearing on this issue. As far as he and the Dirt Diamonds were concerned, they ruled this land.

He pulled back his pantleg and yanked the flare gun from its strap. It was a large weapon, roughly the size of a sawed-off shotgun. He pointed it into the air and squeezed the trigger.

Pearce aimed as he saw the man aim the flare. His shot struck Boyle through the elbow but it was too late. The sizzling ball of fire traveled a mile into the air, trailing red smoke all the way. Then, with a resounding *boom*, it exploded into a huge hot cloud that could be seen for miles.

He took a deep breath, preventing himself from displaying a great deal of anger. He was too late. The main band of Dirt Diamonds had been warned.

CHAPTER 11

A blow to the back of the head knocked Brock to his hands and knees. Usually, he was the one dealing the blow. A muscular man with a height of over six feet, he relished in fierce confrontations with other gangs. He was used to being victorious, beating rival bandits and claiming their goods.

Now, he had to endure the woes of defeat. He and his companions thought they'd take their chances here in Tidal Valley. After traveling a few miles, they spotted a group of people. Brock counted four of them before deciding to raid them. With two buggies, he and his companions raced into action.

Then, seemingly out of nowhere, more appeared.

The skirmish was short and swift. Not only did the enemy have the advantage of numbers, but weaponry as well. Brock and his five companions had pistols and two shotguns.

He stood up on his knees, seeing numerous Dirt Diamonds surrounding him. Never before had he seen such a large gang, much less a gang so heavily armed. The group had circled around him, each member armed with a firearm. Most of the group carried rifles, while others carried heavier weapons.

Laying in front of him were the bodies of his five companions. Three of them had shotgun wounds to the chest. Another had taken a rifle round to the head. The fifth, his girl, had been run over. Her hair was mashed over her pancaked skull, leaving little trace of humanity. The air smelled of charred oil and gas. Their buggies had been smashed and torched. The Dirt Diamonds didn't even take them for scrap metal.

Engines revved as some of the Dirt Diamonds drove around the group. He caught glimpses of them between the bodies of gang members.

The vehicles had a skeletal frame with four large tires. The standard buggies carried four members, while the upgraded ones had a gun mount. There were three upgraded buggies. Two of them carried a mounted flamethrower, while the third had an M60 machine gun turret.

It was that vehicle that ravaged his engine. He had leapt from his buggy before the bullets found their way into the seats, catching one in his leg in the process. His girl wasn't as lucky. As she jumped from the vehicle, she took one in the small of her back, which caused her to faceplant into the dirt. The Dirt Diamonds decided to savor the kill, altering course to drive over her.

Now, he was the only one left.

Someone spoke from behind the wall of bandits. "You've made a grand error in judgement."

Brock looked ahead. The group spaced out, making way for their leader. Brock's pulse quickened as a large muscular man stepped forward. He wore black tactical pants and a sleeveless vest made from wolf skin. He was at least six-foot-three, with biceps almost as large as his head. The eyes were blue, the skin around them marred by several scars. There was a metal mask covering his mouth, held in place by straps that wrapped around the back of his head. Whatever it was, it appeared to serve some type of medical function.

Rarely did the mere sight of a man spark such fear in Brock. He felt himself starting to shake, which caused him to turn his head away.

"You're looking away," the masked man pointed out. "You're afraid. Afraid of death." Brock forced himself to look back up at the man. He was towering over him now, those blue eyes piercing his soul. "I was contemplating reasons to let you live and function as a member of our society."

"I can!" The words shot out of Brock's throat with heightened enthusiasm.

"You would do that?" the man said. "To the man who killed your woman?"

"She's…" Brock tried to think of the right thing to win over his captor's graces. His mind raced, believing it to be a trick question. Perhaps it was a test of loyalty. If he would join the man who just killed his mate, particularly in these circumstances, perhaps it was a sign that he wasn't a loyal person. "She wasn't my woman! She was with him!" He pointed to the dead companion with the gunshot to the head.

The masked man looked at the dead man then back at Brock.

"You are willing to join the Dirt Diamonds and serve me, Cedoz?"

Cedoz. That was his name. Brock had heard it before. He was a warlord; a man who traveled the wasteland in search of resources, battling other clans for dominance.

"Yes," Brock said. His blood rushed. He could feel a sense of hope building within him. Perhaps he would come out of this alive. The man named Cedoz looked at him with that sharp stare. Brock's stomach started to knot. He felt as though he was being studied.

"Yet, even before you join our family, you have committed your first offense," he said. Brock felt himself starting to shake again. He must be referring to the initial raid that he started, before the rest of the Dirt Diamonds appeared.

"Cedoz, I feel I've already paid the price for attempting to rob your scouts," Brock said. "My people are dead. I no longer have an allegiance to them."

"If only you answered that way before," Cedoz said. Brock paused, confused.

"Before?"

"When you lied about your woman," Cedoz said, his voice deepening into a growl. Brock started to stammer.

"I—I, uh, the girl, she's…"

"I would have forgiven your attack. I would have even forgiven the stupidity that led to the attack. But what you did a moment ago was worse: You lied." Cedoz held out a hand, touching his fingertips to Brock's shoulder. "People who are loyal don't lie. And you have just committed that offense."

"No! I—I…" Brock's plea turned into a muffle as Cedoz cupped one hand over his mouth, while grabbing the back of the head with his other hand. With an effortless twist, Brock's neck popped. He spasmed once before falling to the ground, dead.

"What a shame," Cedoz said, brushing his hands together. "Let us continue our goal of finding clean water. There are more water farms scattered throughout the region and we will find them."

"Cedoz!" one of the men called out. His name was Europe. He wore a white eyepatch over his left eye, which contrasted sharply against his jet-black clothing. He wore a chain over his open leather vest which rattled as he walked. Cedoz could tell that his second-in-command was alarmed.

"What is it, Europe?"

"Look north! To the sky!" Europe said, pointing behind him. All eyes turned and saw the big blot of red in the horizon. It was three miles away at least. Cedoz walked a few steps in front of the large gathering, staring at the anomaly with unblinking eyes. He knew what it meant.

"Your brother, my lord," one of the women said.

"What do you wish to do?" Europe asked. Cedoz stared silently at the cloud.

"There's only one purpose for that flare," he said. "My brother has encountered someone." He turned around and faced the wall of bandits. They stood in a single file line like an organized group of soldiers. Men and women gripped their weapons, keeping the muzzles pointed skyward, as they waited for their leader's instruction. "We have a new mission, brothers and sisters! We are hunting now! Go to the smoke! We will find the one who killed Boyle and punish him with a slow death!"

The group lit up with a resounding roar, followed by their battle cry.

"For Cedoz!"

The Dirt Diamonds disbanded and raced toward their vehicles. Engines roared as buggies, pickup trucks, and motorcycles raced north.

CHAPTER 12

Paul smiled as he saw that his father and aunt were unharmed.

"Oh, thank God," Graf said, breathing heavily. He saw the shotgun in his son's hands. He had never taught him to shoot, yet he held the weapon like a professional. "Where'd you get that?"

"Who cares?" Star said. She turned around and allowed Paul to cut the bindings from her hands and ankles. After rubbing her sore wrists, she knelt by Graf and untied him.

Graf shook his head. "I don't—" his voice trailed off. He knew the hypocrisy of what he was gonna say. He didn't want his son knowing how to shoot guns and kill people. He had shot weapons at foes in the past, resulting in one fatality that haunted him to this day. He didn't want his son to experience that.

But that hope was dead. Worse, the boy seemed unfazed by it, like it was a natural thing. In addition, Graf had to accept the reality of the world they lived in. It was full of evil people who would slaughter his son in a heartbeat. Hell, if not for this mysterious stranger, the devious act would've been done and he would've been forced to watch it.

Graf stood up. They all looked at the stranger with intent to thank him, only to watch in stunned horror as he approached Boyle.

The thug was still alive, his breaths becoming wheezy. He was on his back, his forearm dangling from his elbow. He tried spitting up at Pearce, only for his bloodied saliva to fall back over his face.

He yelled out as the loner pressed a boot to his busted elbow. Pain surged through his body like an electric current.

"I know who you are," Pearce growled. He added pressure to his foot, causing Boyle to squirm. "You're a Dirt Diamond. I know there's more of you."

Boyle's scowl transformed into a smile.

"Yes," he said, giggling. "They're in the territory. And they're coming. I will be avenged."

"How many?"

"A hundred and twelve," Boyle said. He was proud to disclose this information. "Cedoz is the leader. I'm sure you've heard of him. If not, you're going to. He's my brother. You see that flare up there? It's red."

"No shit," Pearce said.

"Our other flares carry black smoke," Boyle said, spitting blood. "The red one is specific to me. You see, Cedoz is my brother. He knows that flare is mine." He chuckled and watched the sky. "Ah, look at that cloud expanding. He's seen it by now, and he's coming with the entire gang. You can't outrun him. This wagon is destroyed, and something tells me you don't have a vehicle. We have buggies and bikes! And a lot of guns. You won't make more than two or three miles before he finds you. Enjoy your walk, Loner! It'll be your last."

Pearce stood silent, absorbing the information. The bandit wasn't lying. Pearce felt intense anger billowing within him. He thought of shooting the bastard in the head.

Then he noticed a rock several yards away. It was a yard wide, flat, and dug several inches into the earth. Perfect hiding place for a tarantula. Pearce grabbed Boyle by his throat and dragged him toward the rock. The bandit squirmed, struggling against his capture.

"I'll enjoy *this* walk," Pearce said. He threw Boyle down against the rock. It shook for a moment then opened like a trapdoor. Boyle's eyes opened wide as the eight-legged arachnid darted out, fangs extended. He squealed as it climbed on him, passing over his face and chest before stinging deep into his belly. Boyle tensed, his teeth chipping as they clenched tightly. He spasmed twice before succumbing to paralysis.

The spider climbed over its prey and began draining blood. Once sufficiently fed, it would lay its eggs in Boyle's body then move on to another nest. The baby spiders would hatch and feed off him, then wander out and find their own hideouts.

Graf had to look away. Though the bandit deserved everything he got and more, it was still a grotesque sight. He watched as Pearce walked past them.

Pearce gave them a quick glance, assessing the probability of them being a threat more than anything else. They seemed harmless enough. He found himself staring longer than he intended. The woman's beauty caught him by surprise. Never before had he seen someone with such clean skin. She wore cowhide pants and boots and had a shirt tied over her chest, exposing her toned midsection. They must have discovered a water supply, enough to bath and freshen their skin and hair. Even her teeth were intact. If the situation was different, Pearce would question them and find out where their camp was. But he reminded himself of the looming threat. He had to move.

In his peripheral vision, he noticed Paul approaching with the shotgun. The alarm in his mind sounded off. *Trust no one!* Pearce turned viciously, his hand gripping his revolver. Paul froze, then took another step. He held the shotgun barrel up and extended it to Pearce.

The loner eased up.

"Keep it. And leave me alone," he said. He continued walking away. Star and Graf looked at each other, then walked after him.

"Hey!" Star said. Pearce didn't acknowledge her. "I just want to thank you for what you did."

"Yes," Graf added. "You saved our lives. You saved my son's life."

"It's becoming a habit," Pearce retorted, not looking back. He examined the bodies of the dead Dirt Diamonds, gathering ammo and weapons. There were some useful finds, including three firebombs and two sticks of dynamite.

Graf started to sweat. His wagon was broken, his oxen dead, and his son's condition was doomed to worsen unless he acted quickly.

"Listen, I know I have no right to ask—"

"You don't," Pearce interrupted.
"—but...we need your help. My boy is sick. He's been bitten by a spider. We've given him medicine which has slowed down the effects, but he's still getting worse."

"I'm not a doctor," Pearce said.

"I know, but I know of one who might help," Graf said. "I would appreciate it if you could escort us there. I don't have much to give other than water, but I—"

Pearce shot him a fierce look.

"Did you not hear what that bastard Dirt Diamond said?"

"Well, I did, but that doesn't change the fact that Paul's sick," Graf said.

"Won't be for long," Pearce said. Graf took a step forward, his gratitude having turned to rage. How could somebody be so cold, even in this world? He felt Star place a hand on his shoulder, calming him.

"Please," she said. "Can we come with you then? Clearly, you know this land better than we do. We've gotten turned around. We know we're close but we're not quite sure which direction to take."

Pearce loaded a fresh magazine into his rifle and chambered a round.

"Use the sun," he said.

"Please," Star said again. "At least take us with you and show us where to hide from these gang members."

Pearce picked up his pack and slung it over his shoulder.

"It's your problem. Not mine. You wanted to stay out of danger? You shouldn't have passed through this place."

Without wasting another word, Pearce turned his back and headed west at a steady jog. Star and Graf looked to each other, neither sure what to do at this point.

"I—" Graf stammered, trying to come up with a suggestion. "What do we do?"

"I don't know," Star said. "Maybe there's a place we can hide around here."

"Even *he's* making a run for it," Graf said, pointing a finger to Pearce. "If he's anxious to leave, then these guys must be deadlier than we can imagine. And they'll be pissed when they see what's happened to these guys."

"They won't know who did it," Star said.

"I don't think it'll make a difference," Graf said. "They'll just kill anyone they come across. It won't matter if it's us or…" Graf glanced in Pearce's direction again. "He's planning on having us take the fall for this!"

Star trembled. "That son of a bitch."

"Great. Just great," Graf said, kicking a stone. He started looking around while trying to think of a solution to their problem. The red cloud lingered overhead like a huge ghost. "We need to get away from here for starters. Grab some water and let's go."

He and Star returned to the wagon, filled up some canteens, then stepped out.

"Let's go south," Star suggested. "We might be able to find the cliff if we go this way." She noticed Paul collecting the leftover firearms from the dead thugs. "PAUL!" she shouted.

"What are you doing?" Graf said.

Paul shouldered the weapon, then nudged his head westward. Like a soldier on patrol, he started hustling after Pearce.

Graf thought about it for a moment. Initially, he resisted the idea. However, it only took a few moments for him to finally face reality; they would never escape the Dirt Diamonds. Their best hopes were with the stranger. He was tactically proficient and had a decent understanding of the landscape.

"He's right. We gotta follow that guy," he said.

"How do we know he won't kill us?" Star said.

"We don't. Fact is, though, we're dead anyway if we wait here," Graf answered.

"I suppose you're right. Are there any more of those weapons lying around?" Star asked.

"Two of them. The guy took most of the magazines but left the guns. Left enough bullets to make it look like we killed these thugs. Let's take 'em anyway just in case."

After gathering supplies, they ventured west, following the loner's trail.

CHAPTER 13

Engines roared as the Dirt Diamonds followed their leader through Tidal Valley, avoiding sandpits and other hazards as they neared the cloud.

Cedoz stood up, ignoring the sting from the hot wind as he scanned the landscape in search for any sign of his scouts.

"Two o'clock," he said. "There's something there. Over a thousand yards out."

"Yes, my lord," the driver said. He cut the wheel to the right. Dust swirled as the pack of Dirt Diamonds converged on the site. They found a wagon in shambles. Two dead oxen were riddled with bullet holes. Several yards beyond the wagon were numerous bodies, all belonging to their scouts.

Cedoz held up a fist, ordering the caravan to a halt. Like a platoon of soldiers, the gang disembarked and secured the area. Several of them branched out and examined the bodies, while Cedoz approached Boyle's body.

Boyle's skin had shriveled due to over a quarter of his blood being drained from the tarantula. It was squatting over his torso, its abdomen bloated after intense feeding. It hissed loudly at the gang members then leapt at the biggest one.

Cedoz swatted his hand, knocking the arachnid to the ground. He stomped his foot down, driving his heel through its head. After killing the spider, he gave one final glance at his brother.

"He disobeyed my orders. He was supposed to scout and alert us. Instead, he took matters into his own hands," he said.

"Does it matter?" Europe asked.

"No. It does not matter," Cedoz said. "It was the one promise we had made to my father; never let a family death go unavenged. And we will honor that commitment."

He started examining the wagon. He tossed aside various belongings, much of which had been ravaged by Boyle's group. He stopped when he found a large metal drum. He put his hand on it to get an idea of its weight. As it tilted, he heard the swishing within.

Cedoz tore the top off and looked inside.

"Water," he announced.

"Water?" one of the men asked.

"How much, my lord?"

"Gallons!" He lifted the drum and lowered it to his people, along with a scoop. "Pass it along. Hydrate yourselves. Do it quickly, because we have to move!"

"My lord," Europe said, "forgive me for asking, but is this the right time for them to hydrate? We need to find the ones who killed your brother and…fed him to a spider!" Europe's voice was filled with disgust. His loyalty for Cedoz caused him to share his anger.

"We will easily find them," Cedoz said. "Tidal Valley is not heavily inhabited. Anyone we find within a couple miles will likely be the perpetrator. All we need to do is search hard enough."

Cedoz walked out to the other fallen Dirt Diamonds and examined the ground.

"Whoever did this could not have gone far," he said. One of the female Diamonds explored the land between the bodies. Her name was Lassa, by far the most beautiful member of the Dirt Diamonds. Her beauty was matched only by her fierceness, as well as love for Lord Cedoz.

"We have tracks," Lassa said. "They go west. They're not old."

"They knew what the flare meant; they knew we were coming," Cedoz said. "Keep west. It won't be long until we catch up to them."

"Should we kill them on the spot?" Europe asked.

"No," Cedoz said. "We will not kill them. At least, not all of them." He looked back at the group drinking from the drum of water. "That's more water than we've found in the past month. These people have found a spring. We need them alive to make them tell us where it is. Once we have the location, we will take it for ourselves. Consider it a new base of operations."

"Yes, Lord Cedoz," Lassa said.

The group drank from the water until there was hardly any remaining. They made way for their lord as he approached. Out of respect, they each turned their backs as he lifted his mask from his face. Water trickled through the gap in his lower jaw as he drained what remained, leaving a scoopful for his dear Lassa. He replaced his mask and extended it to her, which she accepted and drank.

Cedoz wanted his warriors healthy. It was a priority to keep them well fed and hydrated. It gave them incentive to remain loyal, as well as kept them in fit enough condition to do his bidding.

"Back in the vehicles," he ordered. The Dirt Diamonds did as commanded. As before, they followed the lead of Cedoz's black semi-truck. They headed west, following the trail Lassa had found.

CHAPTER 14

Pearce gradually increased his pace as he headed west, listening carefully to his surroundings. So far, there were no signs of the Dirt Diamonds. But that could change in an instant. He knew he would not escape by simply running out of Tidal Valley.

It took over a half hour of hard running before Pearce reached the old fort he had found the previous day. He slowed down, carefully avoiding the sandpit that was nearby. The plan was to wait here and see if he would be passed by any mobile patrols. If any group drew too close, he would travel through the water tunnels under the ground.

Catching his breath, he walked to the fort and set his belongings inside. He studied the surrounding terrain as well as the fort itself. He had no idea where that water pipe led, if it led anywhere. On top of that, he could only imagine what underground dwelling mutations might have taken refuge in there. Reality set in during that moment; he would likely have to set up a defensive position here if he was discovered.

Pearce checked out the supplies he collected from the Dirt Diamonds. The pack of dynamite had ten sticks. In addition, he had a flare gun with three flares, as well as two stick flares. If he had to make a stand, he would have to rely on more than simply shooting it against a hundred gang members.

He unwrapped the pack of dynamite and separated the sticks. A detonation from just one of these could take out numerous bandits at once. There wasn't enough time to set up a booby trap with these explosives. However, there was an alternative. A well-placed bullet would be enough to discharge the dynamite.

Pearce set one a hundred feet out from the southeast corner and partially buried it in a thin layer of dirt. It was just enough to keep it hidden, while allowing him to line up a direct shot. He marked its position with a chunk of brick. To the Dirt Diamonds, it would be nothing more than just a piece of debris lying about.

Pearce continued another hundred feet out and set up another stick of dynamite roughly ten yards from the sandpit. He then continued around the fort, burying sticks of dynamite within two-hundred feet of the fort. He made sure to mark each one with either a brick or easily identifiable rock. There were two set up from each side of the fort, leaving the loner with two spares.

Pearce was ready to take position in the fort when he sensed that he wasn't alone. He sniffed the air and listened, then lowered his hand to the ground. There was a slight vibration. Not from vehicles but someone on foot. It was a small group, and definitely not the Dirt Diamonds. They would be on motor vehicles.

He turned around and saw the family approaching in the distance. His blood began to simmer. He hoped they would have gone their separate ways. Instead, they had followed him.

Pearce waited, fighting off a temptation to shoot them on the spot.

"There!" the man named Graf exclaimed. Pearce noticed that they carried the rifles from the dead bandits. The closer they got, the worse Pearce's temper flared. Graf and Star, however, were blind to this due to their exhaustion and desperation.

"Thank God," Star said. She held Paul by the hand. The poor boy had trekked a total of five miles this morning alone and was exhausted. Graf caught his breath then approached Pearce to plead his case.

"Listen, we REALLY need your help—"

A punch to the jaw knocked him on his rear.

"Hey!" Star yelled out. She let go of Paul and grabbed for a pistol she took. A kick from Pearce knocked it from her hands. She staggered back, her hands suddenly empty. Pearce threw another kick at Graf. His heel connected with the shotgun and launched it from his hands.

Star, now blinded by anger, came at Pearce with a wide haymaker. The loner caught her arm mid-swing and threw her over his shoulder.

"You fucking bastard," Graf said. "You were going to leave us there to take the rap!" He sprung to his feet and threw a punch. Pearce deflected it with a simple tapping motion, then thrust an elbow into Graf's stomach. The father doubled over, eyes wide with pain as he stumbled backward.

Star was back on her feet. Yelling with rage, she rushed Pearce with her arms out with intent to tackle him. But the loner saw her coming. He grabbed her brother and threw him into her like a ragdoll. The two siblings collided and bonked foreheads. A kick from Pearce struck Graf in the back, driving him into Star and knocking them both to the ground at once.

A metallic snap drew Pearce's attention behind him. Paul had one of the assault rifles pointed at him. The magazine was fully stocked and in place. He shook his head, warning Pearce to not continue the fight.

Instead, the loner approached. Paul backed up nervously. He shook his head with greater significance. If he could still speak, he'd be screaming for Pearce to stop. But he didn't. Pearce was just a few steps away. Now he was within arm's reach!

Paul closed his eyes and squeezed the trigger.

Click.

He opened them back up. The weapon didn't fire! But he'd loaded the magazine! He knew how to do it!

Pearce snatched the weapon from his hands. Paul stood dumbfounded. He didn't move. Instead, he simply stared up at the loner, whom he had just tried to kill. The man was mad.

He and Pearce locked eyes.

"Don't hurt him!" Graf pleaded. Pearce rolled his eyes. He took Paul by the shoulder and moved him closer, then turned the rifle to show him the side of the barrel.

"Nice try, kid. You have the magazine loaded but you forgot to pull back on the cocking lever," he said. He showed him how to do it. "It needs a bullet in chamber in order to fire and load the next round. Now it's ready to shoot." He tossed the gun back to Paul.

Paul examined the mechanism. There was an energy to him as he tested it. He looked back up at Pearce and smiled, happy to have learned something new.

Pearce couldn't help but appreciate the boy's tenacity. The kid was a survivor at heart, though his tendencies had gotten him into trouble more than once.

Pearce turned to face the adults, who were now back on their feet.

"Why'd you follow me?"

"Why'd you leave us?" Graf retorted.

"Leave you? I have no responsibility for you."

"I don't get it," Star said. "Why'd you help us then?"

"I never helped you," Pearce said.

"You saved us back there, only to leave us to be killed," Star said.

"I didn't save you," Pearce snarled. "Your kid led two of them to me. After I killed them, he stole my pack and made me chase him back to you. By then I had no choice but to kill the bastards. What they wanted to do with you was none of my concern. It's actually *because* of you that I'm in this mess at all."

"Still," Graf said. "You were hoping the gang would find us and not search any further."

"Would've suited me," Pearce said. "Doesn't mean you couldn't have gone your own way."

"Those people are coming," Graf said. "We need your help."

"No."

"Please," Star said. "We have water. We can give you some."

"Already got some," Pearce said. He walked past them to the building. "Besides, going back to your drum would be suicide."

"No, I meant we could lead you back to our camp," Star said. Pearce stopped and looked back. Star could tell by his look that he was waiting for more information. "We've found a water source. We have a small village. A true community centered around this water farm."

"Most water farms are lucky to get a bottle full of moisture a day," Pearce said. "How much is yours drawing?"

"You saw that drum," Graf said. "That was an hour's worth of labor."

"We've set up windmills to power the farm," Star said. "It's enough to keep the machine operating. The community has livestock for food and milk. And that's what it is, a community. We're a peaceful group, making the best of the world we were given. We can take you there. We can make you one of us if you wish. We'll even build you a home."

"Won't be necessary," Pearce said. *Trust no one,* his mind reminded him. Still, he considered their offer. Water was in short supply and he would not be returning frequently to this well to get some.

His thoughts were interrupted by a vibration in the ground. He knelt and felt the earth. He felt the rumblings of heavy machinery that rapidly approached. A moment later, he heard engines and the shouts of numerous violent maniacs.

Star, Graf, and Paul heard it too. Their stomachs tightened as they looked east and saw the enormous band of Dirt Diamonds approaching rapidly.

"Shit," Pearce mumbled. They had been discovered.

"There!" Cedoz yelled. The semi's engine resounded like a behemoth's roar as it drew near the fort. The buggies and motorcycles immediately branched out and began to circle the structure, while several foot soldiers dismounted. The semi came to a screeching halt, less than five hundred feet from the east wall.

"Those are the people we want," Lassa said. She was the first to step out of the truck, followed by the leader. He carried no weapons as he stepped out. Though he had a double-barreled shotgun strapped over his back and a large .500 Magnum revolver strapped to his hip, he allowed his foot soldiers to do most of the shooting.

He was surprised to see the abandoned fort. He had no idea there were any surviving relics of the Revival Wars. Despite the passage of time, it appeared to be in relatively good condition, the majority of its damage appearing to be due to past battles.

His eyes went to the four people standing in front of it. Though they all carried weapons, two of them seemed out of place. Though they held their weapons competently, they didn't have the eyes of killers. The boy even had a more menacing look than them.

Then there was the man in the tactical vest. Cedoz looked at him and the man looked back. *This man* had no qualms about taking life. In fact, he was probably the only person in this group that posed an actual threat.

"*He* killed Boyle," Cedoz said.

Pearce saw Cedoz step out, accompanied by six of his men and one well-shaped woman with dark hair. Battle cries resounded as several men disembarked from their vehicles. Never had Pearce seen so many rifles. This group had been stocking up on weapons and fuel for years to be this well supplied.

"Damn it," Pearce said, watching the leader point directly at him. He noticed the family looking at him, as though awaiting instructions. Star and Graf were visibly terrified. The boy, Paul, started backing toward the structure. He kept the muzzle of his rifle pointed at the group.

The loner bit his lip and silently cursed the family for putting him in this predicament.

"Get inside," he said. He led them around the south wall and ran inside. "Get whatever brick you can and start barricading that breach," he ordered.

"Okay," Star said. She and Graf went right to work, pushing whatever debris they could toward the open gap. Motorcycles zipped within a few feet, causing the pair to stop.

"Keep going," Pearce said. "They're not attacking yet. They're getting a view from inside and reporting it to the big boss up by the semi." They continued rolling large chunks of brick to the side, while Pearce took position by one of the gunner's loopholes. He watched for his markers. So far, they seemed to go unnoticed by the gang.

Buggies roared as they circled the structure, guiding several foot soldiers as they surrounded the building. They maintained a distance of three hundred feet. Not a single one had fired a shot yet. This was enough for Pearce to know that Cedoz wanted them alive, or at least one of them. He was creating an intimidation factor, in hopes that Pearce and these people would surrender out of fear.

Graf and Star groaned as they rolled a huge chunk of wall toward the gap. The pile of debris was now over three feet high, completely blocking the entrance. They peeked outside, seeing Dirt Diamonds all around. Men and women were hustling on foot, while others raced on bikes and buggies. It was like they were trapped in the middle of a vortex of people.

"Will this even hold them off?" Graf asked.

"Hardly," Pearce said. "We just need it high enough to slow them down." He watched the leader as someone handed him a bullhorn. The negotiation phase was moments away.

In the corner of his eye, Pearce saw Paul looking out the south wall. He was trembling with nervousness, his finger resting on the trigger of his rifle.

"Hold up, soldier," Pearce said to him. Paul looked over as the loner approached and demonstrated proper grip with the rifle. "Aim down these iron-sights. Line the center notch with what you want to shoot. Now," he flipped the frame lever, "this sets it to semi-automatic, which means it'll shoot one time when you press the trigger. Now look out there." Pearce pointed out to where he set the dynamite. "See that funny looking rock that looks like a big mushroom?"

Paul nodded.

"Under the ground, right to its left, is a piece of dynamite. When enough bad people get near it, shoot it."

Paul nodded.

"You aren't seriously expecting my son to hold his own in a gunfight, are you?" Graf said.

"After surviving this long with you as a parent, I wouldn't put much past him," Pearce said. He tossed the spare rifles to him and Star. "You can't protect him forever. It's parents like you that get your kids trapped in lizard pits…or bitten by spiders."

Graf swallowed hard. There was no time to get angry. The truth was, the stranger was right.

A booming voice drew their focus back outside.

"There is a phrase from the past: *Fish in a barrel.* That's what you have reduced yourselves to. You are trapped. Like the fish, there is no survival outside that barrier. And like the fish, your time in there is running out."

Cedoz's voice had a mechanical element to it, probably due to that mask he wore. Pearce watched as several gang members worked their way toward the south wall. They knew that was the fort's weakest point, thanks to the bikers' reconnaissance. It was more evidence that they wanted to invade and not demolish. If that scout team carried dynamite, Pearce could assume that this main band carried heavier artillery which they could easily use.

Pearce steadied himself. He carefully watched his markers and the distance that the gang maintained. They just needed to come a little closer.

"I will make you an offer," Cedoz continued. "I am here to avenge my men. However, I suspect that only ONE of you is responsible, as remarkable as that is. Surrender the warrior! Have him step out. And I will let the rest of you live!"

Suddenly, everything went silent. Not a word was spoken, nor an engine revved. It was as though the whole world was waiting on the group's response.

Pearce slowly turned his head until he could see Graf and Star. That voice saying *trust no one*, was sounding off in his mind again. He grew tense. A sixth sense in his brain detected contemplation in the group, especially the father. He regretted returning their rifles. Worse, he regretted leaving them with anything back at the wagon.

He prepared to turn. If he moved fast enough, he would be able to kill them both before they could squeeze off a shot.

"NO!" Star yelled, breathing intensely. She marched to the loophole so she could be heard better. "NO!" she shouted again. She looked back at Graf, who was visibly conflicted. "We're better than that. We don't sacrifice people!" He nodded, breathing nervously.

"I will not make this offer again," Cedoz said. "It is foolish of you to try and resist. You are drastically outnumbered with no way out. My brother is dead, and I am generously willing to allow only one of you to suffer the immediate consequences. But if not, then greater punishment lies ahead for all of you."

Pearce groaned. He'd had enough of the psychological warfare. He rested his rifle barrel along the edge of the loophole and looked down the sights. He could see Cedoz, still over five hundred feet out. He set the lever to semi-auto and steadied his aim.

He squeezed the trigger.

Just then, wind kicked up, driving the bullet to the left.

Blood splattered as the bullet struck one of the men standing beside Cedoz, causing him to abruptly end his monologue. The leader looked at his fallen subordinate, then back at the fort. Even at five hundred feet, Pearce could see the flare in his eyes.

"Have it your way," Cedoz growled. He raised a fist and signaled the attack.

CHAPTER 15

Bullets struck the fort on all sides as the Dirt Diamonds shot from range. A buggy with a mounted machine gun circled the structure like a shark, firing bursts of ammo toward the loopholes. Black dust exploded with each bullet hit, disorientating Star, Graf, and Paul.

Pearce kept his head down as a few shots struck along the edge of his loophole. He waited for the buggy to come around the east side. It finally appeared, keeping about two hundred feet away.

Pearce fired numerous shots, hitting the exoskeleton but missing the passengers inside. Machine gun fire drove him back down. The vehicle continued its circle, hitting the south side, then west.

"Converge on the north wall," Cedoz ordered. The bandits began moving in on foot, led by several men on bikes. Several of them fired at the fort, their bullets fixed on the loopholes. Some passed through, kicking up dust as they struck somewhere inside.

Star was on the verge of panic. She held her rifle close to her chest and summoned the courage to fire. Finally, she moved to the north wall and sprayed several shots out. There were over a dozen bandits, each about two hundred feet away and closing. They spread out as they heard her gunshots. Bullets struck dirt, missing every thug in the grouping.

"Get back!" Pearce ordered. He pulled her back by the shoulder and took her spot. He aimed and fired a single round. The bullet struck one of the thugs in the abdomen. The man froze, his weapon falling from his hands as he looked down and saw the blood spilling from his midsection. He teetered forward like a plank of wood and smashed into the dirt.

Pearce fired another shot, hitting another in the chest. Blood exploded out his back as the bullet punched through his spine. The loner fired a few more rounds before being forced to duck back.

Finally, he could hear the buggy coming around. Machine gun fire struck the northwest corner as it came into view. Pearce raised his rifle again and lined his sights with the black brick marker he had set near a piece of dynamite. The buggy turned the corner, passing only within a hundred feet of the fort. It was too far from the trap.

"Shoot it!" Pearce ordered Graf and Star. They hesitated briefly, then rushed to the loophole and fired wildly. Bullets struck around the already battered windshield, forcing the driver to veer away slightly. The timing and distance were perfect. Pearce fired repeatedly until one of his rounds struck the dynamite stick.

Like an eruption from the dawn of time, the ground burst directly underneath the buggy. The vehicle was launched from the ground. It flipped twice in midair, spraying fragments like shrapnel until it smashed several yards away. Confused and disoriented, the bandits ducked their heads and scattered to avoid the devastation.

With his rifle freshly loaded and set to full-auto, Pearce fired into the jumbled crowd. Bullets ripped through flesh and bone. Dirt Diamonds danced in place as they took rounds to the chest and shoulders. One tried to fire back, only to take a round to the head.

Another went for the wreckage, seeing that the M60 machine gun was intact. Pearce followed the thug with his aim and fired, placing rounds through his waist.

There were men converging on the west side now. Pearce switched to a different loophole. He felt the vibrations of bullets striking the walls as he took firing position. Dust fell around him, forming a thick black fog inside the fort. He fired a burst of rounds into one of the nearest thugs. A pink cloud burst from the man's upper chest as he jerked in a violent, twisting motion. As he collapsed dead, Pearce fired a few rounds over his body into a female thug. The bullets shredded her waist, nearly splitting her in half.

Now the west wall was alive with reverberations. Gunshots rattled the wall, forcing Pearce to duck briefly. He had seconds before they closed in. Their footsteps were like an enormous drum that battered the earth. They quickly grew louder with the gang's approach.

Pearce forced himself back to the loophole. He searched briefly, locating his marker just a yard or so behind the front line of foot soldiers. Bullets struck within inches as he steadied the muzzle. There was no time for precise aim. He fired at full auto, his rounds striking a duo of bandits before striking the dynamite.

An explosion roared, sending bodies hurling for several yards. Body parts flew in all directions, causing the nearby thugs to scatter chaotically. As the thugs spread out, they ceased firing, allowing Pearce to take more precise aim. He fired in short controlled bursts, slaughtering enemy combatants one after another.

"What are you?!" one of the thugs yelled. Pearce didn't answer with words, but with a shot to the jaw. The impact flipped the man back head over heel, sending him crashing facedown into the blood-soaked dirt.

The explosions had caused the forces on the other sides to hesitate. Several men and women had advanced within a hundred feet, only to stop at the realization that there could be explosive traps anywhere.

Paul had missed his first few shots. He had allowed himself to get anxious under stress, which caused his aim to falter. His only successful shot was a hit to the arm. The way the Diamond reacted, he thought he performed a fatal injury, then realized he had simply wounded the man.

But their advance had slowed. Many of them were looking around cautiously in search of traps. Paul realized this was the opportunity to hit the dynamite.

He saw the oddly shaped rock. There were three Diamonds standing near it, each oblivious to what was buried inches from their feet. He looked down the sights, lined the center notch with the spot, then fired.

The first shot went wide to the left. He fired again, this time hitting the foot of one of the bandits. His third shot hit the rock itself.

Finally, his fourth round hit the mark. Instead of a small burst of grey dust, he heard a deafening blast that launched the three bandits several yards. Several thugs backtracked, while trucks and buggies started collecting some of the personnel.

Paul remembered there was another marker to the right somewhere. He located it and smiled, realizing there was a pickup truck with two armed men in the bed. Paul emptied his magazine into the ground near the rock until one of his rounds hit the dynamite stick. The explosion caught the bed of the truck, causing the vehicle to flip forward. The men were hurtled through the air, their weapons discharging in their hands as they flailed.

As they retreated around to the east, Pearce took aim, finding the brick marker in his sights. Several men ran across the field, unknowingly stumbling across his trap. He fired, detonating the stick. Its explosion shook the ground, shredding four Dirt Diamonds into unrecognizable heaps.

"Who in the Seven Seas is this man?!" Europe yelled angrily. He watched the truck smash down, its tailgate pancaking another of their Diamonds in the process. As it did, he saw another group get consumed by another blast. A wave of heat struck him and the leader as they supervised the attack.

A wall of dust struck him and Cedoz. Despite the sting, the leader watched with unblinking eyes, feeling a combination of anger, grief, and admiration. He never thought such a small group could present a challenge on this scale. The warrior side to him even managed to appreciate it.

That's also where the anger came in. He was watching his people being slaughtered. At least twenty of his people had been killed so far, and yet, there hadn't been a single casualty inflicted on the enemy. The warrior had set numerous dynamite traps around the fort, and Cedoz had no way of knowing how many more there were.

Just then, another explosion erupted less than two hundred feet away. Two more Diamonds were hurled from the explosion, their bodies coming apart in midair.

Now the anger was overpowering the admiration.

"Have our people withdraw," he said. He spoke with ease, as though not bothered a bit by the losses.

"Withdraw? You want us to retreat?" Europe asked.

"No," Cedoz said. "But I'm not going to waste any more time and resources on capturing them alive. Prepare the rocket launchers. We will bury them in their fortress."

"As you wish, my lord," Europe said. He blew into a horn, generating a deep sound that signaled to the entire band of Dirt Diamonds to draw back.

Pearce reloaded his rifle while Graf and Star fired several rounds at Diamonds near the north wall. Many of their shots missed as they were continuously forced to duck for cover from enemy gunshots. Then the sound echoed overhead, drawing the men back.

"What's going on?" Star asked. Pearce didn't answer. He watched the gang take new formations. The dynamite defenses had successfully made them wary. All of the dynamite had already been detonated, leaving him with his two spares, though the Dirt Diamonds had no way of knowing that. Pearce watched as they drew back several hundred feet. The fort was still surrounded, with a few trucks weaving between the men.

The trucks stopped numerous times. When they did, one of the bandits would hand something off from the bed to one of the ground troops, then ride off again. Pearce dug his binoculars from the bag and watched one of the exchanges.

The man in the truck bed was handing out RPGs and bazookas.

"They've pulled back," Graf said. "Are they giving up?"

"Not hardly," Pearce said. He looked to the west and south, seeing Diamonds armed with artillery taking aim at the fort. Pearce jumped back from the wall as one of them fired from the east. The RPG struck ten feet above his head, sending huge chunks of brick spilling inward. Pearce snatched his pack to keep it from getting crushed. Another explosion shook the building, nearly bringing the entire east wall down.

Star and Graf fell to their knees. Their ears were ringing and their vision was clouded by dust. Paul staggered back, unsure of what to do. Pearce grabbed him by the back of his shirt and yanked him into the center of the building. A moment later, another explosion burst the wall where he had been standing. With nothing to support it, the section of wall above the desolated ground level collapsed.

Pearce guided Paul into the center of the room then shoved his pack into his hands.

"You lose this, I swear I'll feed you to these guys," he said. Paul put the pack over his shoulder while Pearce dug several pieces of debris from the center. After a few moments, he uncovered a metal hatch. He pushed it open then guided the disoriented Star and Graf over to it. "Get in."

Star wasted no time climbing down the ladder. Graf pushed Paul ahead of him, letting him go first.

"A water pipe?" he asked. "I suppose you know where this leads…"

"Not a clue," Pearce said, shoving Graf down the hatch. Several more explosions shook the building. Pearce fell to his knees, the shockwave causing the hatch door to shut. As he tried to open it again, another blast struck the base of the west wall, sending a wall of smoke and dust sweeping over him.

Pearce brushed his hand over his face to create a few inches of breathable air. As he did, he heard a loud crumbling sound. The wall teetered inward, the bricks coming apart as it collapsed. Pearce turned and dove out of the way. The wall fell halfway until its top smashed into the east wall. Leaning at a forty-five-degree angle, the wall broke apart piece by piece. Debris crashed down around him, burying the hatch.

He pushed to his feet, only for a chunk of brick to crash between his shoulders and knock him back to the floor. He rolled to his left, avoiding an even larger piece from sandwiching him. Debris rained down until the wall disintegrated entirely, covering the floor of the building in rubble.

Pearce spat up dust as he stood up. He moved carefully to the southeast corner to measure the threat, using the dust cloud to keep himself obscured from view.

The Dirt Diamonds were cheering victoriously with many of them starting to close in on the fort.

"Go in and finish them off, if there are any still alive," Cedoz called out, his voice still as mechanical sounding as before.

Pearce saw the rubble covering the hatch. There was one particularly large piece weighing it down. Just by looking at it, he knew it would take a few tries for him to move it. He needed to find a way to slow down the gang to buy time.

He glanced out through one of the cracks in the east wall. A wall of foot soldiers were moving in, being cautious enough to steer clear of the sandpit.

Pearce checked the distance. As he had estimated the day prior, the pit was three hundred feet from the southeast corner. An idea came to mind.

He dug one of the spare dynamite sticks from his vest and broke away a section of fuse, leaving roughly five seconds' worth attached. With the lighter he took from Paul, he lit the tip then stepped through the breach to allow himself a good clean throw.

"We have a breather!" one of the Diamonds shouted. Several weapons pointed at him.

Pearce chucked the dynamite then dove back into the building as bullets struck all around him. After landing on his stomach, he army-crawled back toward the hatch.

The dynamite hit the ground and bounced once, settling less than a yard from the sandpit. It detonated, causing minor delay for the nearby Diamonds. There was not a single casualty as a result of the explosion, which caused some of them to laugh.

"He's getting desperate," one of them said.

"Here I was thinking he knew what he was doing!" another laughed. The remark was met with laughter from his companions.

That laughter subsided as the men heard a rumbling in the ground. Something was causing the earth to vibrate. Every Diamond near the south and east side stopped and looked toward the pit. The sand erupted, followed by two enormous grey pincers.

An enormous scorpion with a body length of sixteen-feet launched itself from its hideout. Its many eyes saw the smorgasbord of soft meat prey all around it. The Dirt Diamonds shrieked in horror as they retreated in various directions. The charcoal-colored arachnid hissed and began its assault. Its many legs punctured the dirt as the creature scurried with frightening speed to the nearest prey.

Both claws reached out, catching one of the men by the shoulders and feet. Without hesitation, the tail lashed. The Diamond yelled as the tip of the barb punched into his lower back. The venom's effect was instantaneous, rendering him permanently paralyzed.

Opting to collect more prey and feed later, the scorpion tossed him aside and darted for the next target.

A female Diamond yelled as it closed in on her. She emptied her magazine into it, the bullets ricocheting from its hard shell. The claws snatched her up and raised her high. The tail struck, imbedding the barb in her midsection. The scorpion tossed the paralyzed victim away and lashed for the next one.

Pearce looked back, seeing the creature's shape through the cloud of dust. The air was full of screams and gunfire as the gang fought against the arachnid. Several other thugs ran from around the north and west side to assist in the effort to put the creature down.

Pearce stood up and hurried to the hatch. The slab of wall was over a foot thick and as long as a door. He put his weight against it and pushed to the left. The slab moved only a few inches. Pearce took a breath and pushed a second time, grinding it another few inches. He could see the metal hatch exposed underneath.

He heard the sound of crunching rubble near the south wall. Three Diamonds entered the fort through the gap, their fingers resting on the triggers of shotguns and rifles. Their faces bared teeth as they aimed their weapons to shoot.

With a robotic instinct that seemed to engage automatically, Pearce drew his .357 Magnum revolver and fired three times. Each bullet struck home square in the chest, dropping all three combatants.

There was more movement, this time coming from behind him. He turned around to face the north wall. Two shooters had climbed over the debris pile and pointed their rifles. Pearce jumped to his left as they fired. Bullets whizzed past him, one of them grazing his shoulder. He fired back with his revolver, his shot striking one of them in the ribcage. The bandit descended into a spin, his rifle barrel accidentally striking his companion, knocking him backward. Pearce fired his last two rounds. One struck the same thug in the back, finishing him off, while the second punched through the other's neck.

Pearce reloaded the revolver, took one of the assault rifles, then slammed himself against the ledge. He needed to move it another eighteen inches before he could clear the hatch.

"Get back, my lord!" Europe warned Cedoz as the giant scorpion moved toward the semi-truck. Thugs circled the creature, hitting it with everything they had. Bullets crunched uselessly against its shell as it grabbed another Diamond. The thug screamed as the pincers sawed through his flesh. The claws pulled away from each other, each holding a segment of the victim. Entrails rained down from the two halves before being fed into the jaws.

The creature turned, its tail lashing like a whip. It struck another victim and sent him skyward, his body separating at the waist in midair.

An RPG struck its shell behind the head. The creature fell onto its belly, the shell cracked along its back. However, it still held. The beast pushed itself back on all eight legs then turned around. The shooter frantically attempted to reload, only to scream in horror as the arachnid darted for him. It lashed out with one of its claws, slicing him across from the shoulder to hip. Blood pooled at his feet as his body fell apart.

The creature had gone haywire, no longer killing for prey, but to satisfy a bloodlust.

"There's dynamite in the supply truck. Grab me a few stacks," Cedoz ordered.

"But my lord…" Europe said.

"Don't question me!" Cedoz snapped.

"Yes sir," Europe said. He dashed to the back of the convoy where one of the supply trucks was parked. A man on the bed handed him three stacks of dynamite, each consisting of six sticks held together by electrical tape. Europe returned to the leader and handed him the explosives.

Cedoz strapped two to his vest, lit the twelve-inch fuse on the third, and raced toward the scorpion.

"Lassa, draw its attention. Get it to turn its back toward me," he said.

"Yes, my love!" Lassa responded. She dashed to the left as the scorpion grabbed another Diamond and pulled him apart with its claws. She aimed for its eyes and fired. The bullets struck along its face, causing the creature to turn toward her. It extended its claws and started moving in toward her.

Cedoz was in position. He knelt down and aimed for the crack along the scorpion's back. With every ounce of strength he could muster, he threw the stack. It came down in a steep arch, its sparkling fuse giving it the appearance of a meteorite. He had timed it perfectly; it struck the creature's back, right as the fuse burnt down into the center stick. A fiery explosion launched chunks of shell from its body, each piece trailing thick globs of blood. The scorpion fell on its stomach again. Its tail lashed blindly while its claws and legs flailed. It was still alive.

The leader grabbed his double-barreled shotgun and ran at the creature. He ducked to avoid a slash from its tail, then closed the distance. He climbed between two of the flailing legs until he was all the way up on its back. He found the gaping wound behind its head then slammed the shotgun into the soft flesh below. He fired both barrels, causing blood and guts to spew from the wound.

The scorpion spasmed, then curled into its deathly pose.

The Dirt Diamonds caught their breath and surrounded the beast. For a moment, it seemed they had forgotten the reason they were here. They stared at their leader in awe, mesmerized by the feat he had accomplished.

Cedoz looked back at his people, then at the numerous bodies that had begun their decay in the dirt. His gaze moved to the desolated fort.

"Let's finish this."

Pearce threw his body against the slab with all his might. The brick scraped against the metal hatch as it nudged several inches. He hit it again, while listening to the chaos taking place outside. There were a couple of explosions followed by shotgun fire. What came after that bothered him the most: silence.

The creature was dead. He had to escape now, or else find himself at the hands of the gang. Pearce pressed his hands against the corner and dug his feet into the ground. The rubble moved with gradual pace. Sweat rolled down his face in thick beads.

He could hear several bandits running toward the fort. With moments left, he laid into the brick, moving it another few inches. Finally, he saw the opposite edge of the hatch. He lifted it up and descended down the ladder.

Several thugs swarmed the building, led by Cedoz's second-in-command.

"THERE!" Europe yelled. Pearce pulled the hatch shut, feeling the vibrations of a dozen bullets striking it from the outside. He twisted the wheel, locking it from inside.

Europe and his men converged on the hatch. He pulled up on it, only to realize it was sealed.

"Damn!" he yelled, kicking it. Cedoz entered the building with Lassa at his side. "He went down here, my lord! It's a hatch leading to some sort of underground passageway."

"Can it be opened?" Cedoz asked.

"It's locked. There must be a lever or something on the inside," Europe answered.

"Then we will take more drastic measures," Cedoz said. "Get some dynamite charges. We will blow it open."

CHAPTER 16

Pearce splashed into the little stream below after sliding down the ladder. With the hatch sealed, he was trapped in darkness. His hands fumbled over his vest in search of anything to generate light.

"There he is!"

The beam from a flashlight engulfed him. Pearce raised his fists, then settled after recognizing the family.

"We thought they killed you," Star said. Pearce stared at them, confused. Why would they stay and wait for him? They looked up, hearing movement from above.

"No time to waste," Pearce said, his voice hoarse from the smoke and dust. He took the flashlight from Paul and led them down the corridor. The water and metal walls bounced the white light back at him, revealing a long narrow corridor. From where they stood there didn't appear to be an end in sight.

"What is this place?" Graf asked.

"It was probably constructed before the nuclear war. I'm assuming somebody found it during the Revival Wars and wanted it for themselves, so they decided to fortify a defense."

"Is there a way out?" Star asked.

"We'll probably find one if we keep searching," Pearce said. "Come on."

The family followed him as he moved down the corridor.

****

Europe strapped five sticks of dynamite together and placed it near the hatch. His white eyepatch had turned black from the dust, as had his skin. He glanced back, making sure the rest of the gang was out of the blast radius.

He lit the twelve-inch-long fuse and dashed out of the structure. The fire sparked as it ate its way down the wick. The dynamite exploded, toppling the standing remains of the fort. Dust and fire swirled into a giant vortex that twisted high into the sky.

****

Pearce and the family looked back as the explosion echoed through the corridor.

"Oh, God," Star said. "What's just happened?"

"They've exploded the hatch. They're following us," Pearce explained. He dimmed the flashlight to its minimum illumination. "We've got to move fast." They accelerated their pace to a run. After a hundred yards, they came to a bend in the corridor and followed it.

****

Cedoz was the first to approach. He gripped his .500 Magnum revolver and dug through the rubble. The hatch had been blown clean off, the corridor visible below.

"It will be narrow down there," Lassa said. "If too many of us go down, it will be a shooting gallery for that guy."

"She is correct, my lord," Europe said. "Let me go down in your place."

"Take a dozen men with you," Cedoz ordered. "The rest of us will wait here."

"I only need a few to finish the job," Europe said.

"This man has already killed more than a *few*," Cedoz reminded him. "He might not be in the open, but he's proven to be resourceful and dangerous. Also, he knows you're coming."

"We will kill him, my lord," Europe said. "I will avenge your brother and our fallen Dirt Diamonds."

"Do not fail me," Cedoz said. There was a menace in his voice that caused Europe's stomach to briefly tighten. Those blue eyes burned into him, reinforcing the unspoken threat.

"I will not," Europe said. He quickly descended the ladder, followed by twelve Dirt Diamonds. They assembled below and illuminated their flashlights. Europe studied the water, seeing bits of rubble swirling in the tiny stream. "They've been through here. Keep the lights low and follow my lead."

****

Pearce led the group another hundred meters, seeing nothing but dull steel walls with no way out. At the end of that hundred meters, the tunnel began to widen. Pearce adjusted the brightness on his flashlight then shone it directly ahead. Fifty feet ahead, the light caught the edges of what appeared to be the tunnel frame.

There was a juncture ahead.

Pearce stopped and listened. There were footsteps deep in the tunnel behind him, the echoes warping into bizarre sounds as they bounced through water pipes.

"It won't be long until they catch up," Graf whispered. The group continued on until they entered the juncture. They were standing in a large chamber where several tunnels met.

There was a grim appearance to this place, as though it harbored a sinister presence. The air was stale, the water black due to the mineral pollutants. There were pieces of debris lying in the water. Much of it had come from the ceiling. Electrical pipe had been torn as well as fragments from the walls. At first, Pearce assumed the damage was due to shockwaves from the Death Flash. However, there was no consistency to the damage. In fact, it appeared that the debris had not been shaken loose, but rather forcefully torn from place.

There were five other tunnel entrances, two of which were completely caved in. Rock and dirt had smashed through the ceiling, rendering passage impossible. On the contrary, one of the tunnels to the left had been drastically widened. Pearce studied the edges, noticing bizarre grooves that lined the frame. There were three at a time, traveling parallel at a meter's length. Much of the siding had been ripped free, exposing grey layers of soil.

"Something tells me that tunnel wasn't built that way," Pearce said. He wasn't sure what else to make of it, other than that it was the aftermath of a struggle. Whatever had caused it, he didn't want to find out.

There was only one other tunnel.

The footsteps grew louder. Pearce looked back, seeing white lights shining through the bend several hundred feet back. Pearce opened the pack and removed the flare gun and an extra flare.

"This way," he whispered, guiding the group to the tunnel ahead. "Turn off the flashlight."

"You sure we don't want to go this way?"

"For someone who wants me to protect you and your kid, you tend to question my instructions frequently."

Graf nodded. The guy had a point. Without saying anything further, he hurried into the corridor with Star and Paul. The tunnel continued straight for several hundred yards at least; not enough time to get out of sight. Pearce studied the tunnel walls, finding a notch twenty feet in from the juncture.

"Keep going that way. Go and don't stop. You'll eventually come to a ladder that should take you to the surface. And you…" he pointed at Paul, "didn't I tell you to kill that light?!" he reminded Paul. The boy twisted the handle, cloaking the group in darkness.

"What about you?" Star asked.

"I'll wait. I have a surprise for your friends," he said. He watched across the juncture, seeing the light growing brighter as the thugs neared the bend. "Now go."

"One more thing: I never caught your name," she said.

"I didn't give it," Pearce said. He sighed. Apparently, the answer was important to the woman. *Whatever would make her go away.* "Pearce."

"Thank you, Pearce," she said.

"Whatever. Now go," he said. "Wait any longer, they'll see you when they make the turn."

He felt a tightening around his shoulders as Star threw her arms around him, hugged him briefly, then followed her brother and nephew through the tunnel. They kept close to the walls to minimize the amount of splashing caused by their footsteps, which could be heard throughout the corridor.

Pearce waited, his mind stuck on the affectionate gesture.

The raiders turned down the brightness of their flashlights as they turned the corner and closed in on the juncture.

Europe held a hand close to the chain that lined his chest to keep it from rattling. He looked up and studied the wide area. The ceiling was over fifteen feet high, the room itself over twenty feet in width with four other entrances. Two were caved in, one was oddly widened.

He listened carefully, hearing distant footsteps moving down the corridor directly ahead.

"We're getting close," he said.

"Which way did they go, boss?" one of the raiders asked.

"We'll go straight ahead," Europe said. "Let's quicken the pace. We don't want to keep Cedoz waiting. Let's get these guys and give them a taste of what hell is like."

A voice echoed through the juncture. "Why don't you find out for yourself?"

The group stopped and shone their lights through the tunnel entrance, catching a glimpse of the warrior peeking out of a notch in the wall. He had a firearm in hand; a pistol.

Europe noticed the orange color. Not a pistol: a flare gun!

A ball of sizzling hot fire ripped into the juncture, striking one of the raiders in the chest. Inside of a few brief moments, his chest and head were ablaze. Screaming in agony, the raider dropped his weapon and ran wild, lighting the juncture in hot red colors.

Pearce fired his spare, hitting another raider. The same thing happened, giving Pearce full view of his targets while keeping himself hidden in darkness.

"Get him!" Europe yelled.

Gunfire cracked inside the narrow space, causing ears to ring. Pearce hugged the wall tight as bullets whizzed past him. The burning men still screamed and ran wild.

One of them blindly ran into Europe, scalding him with his own burning flesh.

"Get off me!" he snarled. The raider didn't hear him. Sizzling red lights sparked in his eyes, momentarily blinding him. Europe stepped back, pointed his rifle, and shot the man. He splashed down, the water only coming up to his shoulders while his chest still burned.

Europe looked back to the corridor just in time to see the muzzle flashes.

Pearce fired in bursts, his first shots dropping two more of his pursuers. The raiders spread out and returned fire. Bullets struck the wall inches from his head, forcing Pearce to slip into the notch. He stuck the weapon out and blindly fired a few rounds to keep them from rushing the tunnel.

Europe ducked as a couple of rounds zipped near his head. He grew increasingly agitated with each passing moment. The deathly screams of the other burning raider were not helping his concentration. Fed up, Europe turned around and shot the man to death. *It's a mercy anyway,* he thought to himself.

"Move in," he ordered. He pointed to his men to direct them. "You and you, take the left and get some lights on the bastard. I'll take the right and shoot him as you draw him out—"

The flash from a stick flare caught their attention as it was hurtled into the juncture, brightly illuminating Europe and his eight remaining raiders. Waterproof, the flare sank under the water and cast the juncture in flickering red.

"Fuck!" Europe yelled, blindly firing into the side of the corridor, unaware that Pearce had moved to the other wall as they were momentarily blinded by the flare.

He returned fire, hitting a raider standing to Europe's left. The thug doubled over and fell on his face, dead as soon as he touched the water.

Realizing he was next, Europe dove. The next round of bullets passed over him, striking a raider that was standing a couple yards behind him.

Water splashed as Europe raced on all fours to get out of the line of fire. Another of his men rushed the entrance, firing his weapon into the corridor. Every shot streaked by his intended target, whom he could not see until his flashlight panned to the left. Finally, he saw the shooter, and the rifle muzzle pointing at his face.

Pearce fired a single shot, rupturing the raider's skull and dropping him backward.

"Hug the walls," Europe said. "Go along the sides. You'll be out of his line of sight." The group dispersed. Pearce fired several more rounds into the juncture, hitting nothing but water and debris as the Dirt Diamonds moved past his range of vision.

He tossed another stick flare into the juncture, keeping the space lit.

In the juncture, Europe stood with three of his men near the wide tunnel entrance. They slowly worked their way along the circular walls of the juncture, keeping as quiet as possible as they neared the tunnel. Across from him, his two remaining raiders did the same. They were about twenty feet from the tunnel.

Pearce reloaded his rifle and waited. He steadied his breathing to keep it from clouding his hearing. The juncture was dead silent, save for a few random ripples. Listening carefully, he deduced that the ripples were coming from the far sides of the juncture. The raiders were slowly closing in with intent to rush the tunnel.

He felt along his pockets for the last dynamite stick. Holding it in his hand, he waited for the men to get close enough so he could give them a special surprise.

A rumbling interrupted the silence. Pearce peeked around the corner. There was nobody in the tunnel entrance. The ground wasn't moving. It wasn't an earthquake. Rather, it sounded as though a large mass was shifting somewhere in the series of tunnels.

Europe froze as he felt the vibrations. The rumbling was accompanied by scratching sounds, like sharpening knife blades. He turned and looked at the widened tunnel entrance behind him. Dust trickled down from the ceiling as a mass shifted deep within.

"Europe!" one of the raiders called from the opposite side. Europe looked their way, seeing the two men staring wide-eyed at the big tunnel. They pointed their rifles and lit their flashlights, then screamed.

Rubble exploded from the entrance as a huge reptilian beast lunged into the juncture. Twenty feet in length, the creature walked on all fours, its teeth over a foot long. Its head was like that of a dragon, its thick skin covered in razor-sharp spines. Three curved talons extended from each of its feet, each over a meter in length.

The raiders broke into panic as the beast roared. It dove for the flashlights, its skin deflecting gunfire as it lunged for the men with the flashlights. Its jaws closed around one of them and lifted him high into the air. The raider squealed then gurgled as spiked teeth reduced his trunk to minced meat. It chomped repeatedly, completely obliterating his body before swallowing.

"Kill it!" Europe yelled. The raiders opened fire. The beast twitched, not out of pain, but confusion as it felt the bombardment of bullets. Not a single one penetrated its skin.

Its clubbed tail swung in a wide arch. Europe and two others dove out of the way, while the third in his group hesitated. The tail caught him in the chest, pulverizing his entire upper body. The impact flung him across the juncture, sending him smashing into one of the walls.

It focused its attention on the final raider on the right-hand side. The man frantically reloaded, then fired a few more shots, which struck with no effect. The raider turned and ran, only to be swatted by the lizard's huge claw. The talons sliced through his body at the neck, stomach, and groin, throwing all three sections across the juncture.

The beast turned around, its snarling jaws coated in blood. It saw the three remaining prey hitting it with their useless invisible projectiles. It growled, angered from being awakened by their conflict. It had claimed these tunnels as its territory. Anything that dared to set foot inside was subject to its wrath.

Europe emptied his magazine, striking the creature with each round. Yet, it stood unfazed. He reached for a fresh magazine, then stopped as he saw the orange glow radiating from its mouth. Funnels of smoke twirled from the corners of its mouth.

No, he thought. *Such a thing only exists in legends...*

It didn't. The creature reared its head back, its long neck forming an 'S' shape. Europe turned to his right and ran for the back tunnel where they came. The head heaved forward, the jaws hyper-extending. Hot orange fire spewed from its throat, engulfing the final two raiders. The men dropped their weapons and twisted in agony. The flames ate through their bodies like acid, reducing them to charred skeletons within a few seconds.

The intense heat filled the juncture and spilled into the corridor. In the blink of an eye, the temperature had increased to nearly two hundred degrees. Pearce coughed intensely after taking a breath. He felt as though he was breathing in a chemical weapon.

The creature heard the sound of coughing, then lowered itself to gaze into the corridor. Pearce looked over, his eyes locking with those of the beast. It was a true-to-life Fire Lizard, mutated by years of exposure to radioactivity. Once again, its mouth was glowing.

"Oh, shit," he said. Without hesitating, he turned and ran. A river of flame escaped the creature's mouth. The walls lit a bright orange and the air turned hot. Pearce felt the wall of heat on his back as the flame drew near. The stream died down as it reached its maximum range, falling short of its target by mere inches.

The Fire Lizard roared, frustrated. Still running, Pearce glanced back at it.

"You'll have to try harder if you wanna eat me," he said.

The Fire Lizard roared again, then reared back. In a springing motion, it threw itself into the corridor. Its spiny back and shoulders scraped the walls as it pulled itself through the narrow space, while smoke puffed from its nose and mouth.

Pearce sprinted, pushing his legs to the max as he retreated through the dark corridor.

Europe picked himself up from the water and looked back. The creature was no longer on his trail, favoring the loner instead. He watched for a moment to make sure he could get away without attracting its attention. Once its entire body was squeezed into the tunnel, he stood up completely and ran as fast as he could.

As he made his way back, he dreaded the inevitable debriefing that would come as soon as he emerged. With a little luck, Cedoz would be merciful on him. If not, he'd be better off taking his chances with the lizard.

"What the hell is that?" Star felt the rumbling beneath her feet. Graf and Paul felt it too. The father put a hand against the wall. It vibrated in strange rhythms. The sounds of gunfire had been replaced by a dull scraping sound.

Paul turned on the flashlight and aimed it back. Graf pointed the rifle as soon as he saw the man running toward them.

"Pearce!" Star said. Graf aimed the weapon away, relieved that it wasn't a Dirt Diamond. Then he noticed something behind him, something that filled up the entire tunnel. Clawed feet pulled the reptilian body through the tunnel. Its teeth were long and narrow, and nearly black in color. Puffs of flame rolled from its mouth, dissipating into clouds of black smoke.

"Go! RUN!" Pearce yelled.

The family raced through the corridor, splashing water with each step. They followed the tunnel through a series of turns and bends.

The creature's tail smashed side-to-side, ravaging the tunnel as it pushed itself through. It reached its arms out as though climbing a mountain, gaining two to three yards with each motion.

Pearce followed the flashlight beam, seeing a small widening up ahead.

"Another juncture," he said. The group kept at their brisk pace until they cleared the entrance. The juncture was less than half as wide as the previous one. In fact, the only tunnel they saw was a continuation of the one they were currently in. He grabbed the flashlight from Paul and shined it upward. He continued studying the ceiling as they entered the space.

Star passed through the space and into the next corridor entrance. She glanced back, seeing Pearce looking up. Fifty feet behind him was the beast, its eyes glowing red. Drool sizzled between its hot gums as it crawled nearer to the juncture.

"You gonna stick around and sightsee?" she said.

"You can keep running if you want," he responded, moving to the side wall. Star watched the flashlight and realized Pearce had found a ladder leading straight up to the surface. In her eagerness to run, she had missed it entirely.

"God bless you, Pearce," she muttered.

"Hurry up," he said to the family. Star and Graf pushed Paul up the ladder. The boy moved swiftly, finishing the twenty-foot climb within a few moments. Star went up next, with Graf climbing right behind her. The boy twisted the lever and pushed hard on the hatch. Rust flaked off as it opened outward. Bright rays of sunlight blinded him as he stepped out.

The juncture began to shake as the beast's head emerged from the tunnel. Pearce jumped on the ladder and climbed up after them. The creature roared and filled the juncture with flame. The air grew hot as fire passed under Pearce's boots. Star cleared the hatch and was immediately followed by Graf. Star looked back down and extended a hand toward Pearce.

"Come on!" she said.

The creature snarled again, unable to tilt its head high enough to scorch the intruder. It clutched the entrance frame with its claws and pulled itself through.

Pearce ignored Star's gesture and pulled himself free, jumping up from the last ladder bar. Graf pushed the hatch door shut then sat on the hatch.

"Yeah, *that'll* keep it from getting through," Pearce mumbled. Graf thought for a moment, realized the foolishness of his reasoning, and quickly moved away from the hatch. The group listened carefully, hearing the creature circling around in the juncture below.

It moved back and forth a few times. They heard its claws scraping against the ladder, severing some of the bars. The beast growled, then lowered itself from what sounded like an attempt to climb.

After several more moments, there was nothing but silence. The beast had given up.

Pearce untensed his body.

"Never getting water out of there again."

CHAPTER 17

Europe closed his fingers on the ladder bar and slowly hauled himself up through the fort hatch. Cedoz stood in precisely the same spot as when he'd gone down, arms crossed, looking as if he hadn't moved an inch during the entire wait.

Europe stood in front of him, straightened his eye patch, and looked the leader in the eye.

"Where's your crew?" Cedoz said.

"We encountered a mutation," Europe answered. "A flame-spitting beast. It killed my men. I was the only one who survived."

"And what of the subjects?"

"We engaged the warrior, but the firefight must have awakened the beast," Europe said.

"Are they alive?" Lassa asked.

"Unknown," Europe said.

"They are," Cedoz said. "That warrior set a trap for you, Europe. He's cunning and resourceful. You allowed yourself to be tricked."

"No, my lord," Europe protested. "It was just a bad coincidence. I will not be outwitted by a simple wanderer! I'll prove it to you!"

"Prove it to me?" Cedoz was smiling under that mask. "How so?"

"It appears these tunnels travel throughout this wasteland," Europe explained. "There are likely other hatches like this one here. If they escaped the beast, all they would have to do is follow the tunnels until they find one. We can scout, my lord. We'll take the vehicles and travel far and wide until we find them!"

Cedoz narrowed his gaze at Europe.

"Don't let having one eye impair your vision, Europe. It would be very unfortunate for you to lose the other."

"Yes, my lord," Europe said, understanding the threat. He stepped away from the ruins. He saw the remaining band of Dirt Diamonds waiting near their vehicles. He estimated that there were sixty-five of them left, all of them thirsty for revenge.

There was a buggy parked close by. It had a flamethrower platform built up behind the front seats. There was a raider already mounted on the weapon, as well as someone in the passenger seat. "You two are coming with me," Europe said. He climbed aboard the rear and pushed the gunner away from the flamethrower. "You drive."

The raider seated himself at the wheel and started the engine.

"Where to?"

"Head west. We'll find them somewhere," Europe said. He tested the flamethrower, sending brief puffs of fire out the nozzle. The buggy made a U-turn and raced west, while other Dirt Diamonds boarded other trucks to scout in various directions.

****

Pearce remained kneeling by the hatch, listening to the creature's movements below to confirm that it would not attempt to climb out. The family moved several yards away to prevent any of their vibrations from drawing it out. After a few more circling steps, it sounded as though the creature had settled down into a slumber. He got up and regrouped with the family.

"It's given up," he said. "I suspect it was being territorial."

"I've never seen a mutation like that," Star said. "Was it just me, or could that thing actually breathe fire?"

"It breathes fire," Graf confirmed.

"Good Lord Almighty," Star muttered. "I've never seen a mutation like that."

"Then you've hardly set foot outside of that community of yours," Pearce said.

"Where did it come from? Was it living in the tunnels?"

"Something like that," Pearce said. He listened to the creature some more then finally stepped away from the hatch. He gazed at the terrain around them. There were ravaged remains of some sort of small town. Cars laid half-buried in the dirt, some embedded in the decaying structures of old houses and shops. Beyond the area was nothing but countryside, having turned a greyish-brown since the Death Flash. Judging by his surroundings, Pearce estimated that they had traveled nearly two miles from the fort. He saw some rolling hills to the northeast and a line of rock structures to the south, but overall, he didn't recognize this patch of land.

Most importantly, there were no signs of the Dirt Diamonds anywhere.

With them being out of danger at the moment, Pearce thought of the reason he was out here in Tidal Valley to begin with. The boy, Paul, was sitting down on the rock, still wearing the pack.

Pearce stepped over to him and snapped his fingers to get his attention.

"Give it here," he said. Paul was slow to start taking it off. Impatient, Pearce yanked the pack off of him. He dug the syringe out, then cursed aloud after inspecting it. During the skirmishes, the protective cap had come off. The vial was in good condition but the needle was broken.

Star quickly approached, her face displaying concern.

"What is it?"

"Not your concern," Pearce said. Star raised her hands defensively.

"I don't mean to come off like I'm trying to pry. I just want to know if I can help in any way?" She tilted her head to get a look at what he was holding. She saw the glass vial filled with a red liquid. "You're not a drug user, are you?" She was immediately answered with a piercing glare. "Okay, you're not."

Pearce placed the syringe back into his pack, then started walking west.

"Where are we going?" Graf asked.

"*You* can go whichever way you please," Pearce said. "*I'm* getting out of here while I can."

"Remember our deal! You help us, we give you water," Graf reminded him. Pearce continued walking, not even bothering to glance back.

"I never agreed to any deal," he said.

Graf clenched his fist, angry and desperate at the same time. His face was tense, as was Star's. However, they knew they couldn't force the loner to help. Even if they tried, it would be their undoing.

Graf looked at the sun to determine which direction they needed to go. By his estimates, they needed to go south.

"Alright, get your stuff together and let's....Paul, you okay?" Graf said. He rushed to his son, who was leaning heavily to the side. Paul had turned pale, his lips with a tint of purple. The veins in his neck were discolored and his eyes were slightly bloodshot.

"Oh God," Star said, rushing by his side. She checked his pulse. It was normal, though in an hour's time she knew it would start to decrease.

Pearce could hear the distress in their voices.

Just keep walking, he thought to himself. *Not your concern.*

"The infection's really getting bad," she said. Graf fought to keep himself from welling up. He could not let his son see him in distress. Internally, he was screaming at himself, *this is your fault, you idiot! You waited too long. You should've made this journey right after he got bit!*

"I know!" he snapped. He immediately noticed Star staring at him, taken aback. He realized she thought he was directly responding to her. "Sorry, uh… We have to get him help." He stood up and ran to catch up with Pearce. He turned and stood in his way, stopping him. "Please, I'm begging you. We need to get to a water farm."

"I thought you came from a water farm," Pearce said.

"No, there's one out here. Our father lives out here. He's a doctor. He should be out here with our other sister, who rode out here ahead of us to alert him."

"Your father lives out here?" Pearce asked.

"Y-yeah," Graf said.

"Old man? Dark cloak? White beard?" Pearce continued.

Graf came alive with excitement. "Yes! That's him! You know where he is!"

"He's dead," Pearce said. Graf's jaw dropped, his newfound energy instantly evaporated. He stumbled backward as though dealt a physical blow to the gut.

"De—what? How do you know?"

"What happened?" Star said.

"Saw the water farm surrounded by a large gang of thugs. Same ones that are chasing us now," Pearce said. "I saw it from the cliff edge. Knowing this group, they probably didn't let them live after they finished raiding the farm."

"Wait? You don't know for sure he was dead?"

"Even if he's alive, any supplies he had are certainly gone. The Dirt Diamonds take *everything*."

Graf felt himself getting dizzy. His legs shook then gave out, dropping him to the ground. Star rushed to his side. It was obvious that her brother was overwhelmed with shock. She hugged him close, then looked up at Pearce, her eyes welling with tears.

"Just take us there," she said. "We'll give you all the water you want."

"Means nothing to me," Pearce said. "In case you haven't figured it out, those Dirt Diamonds aren't done looking for us. They'll tear this entire desert apart until they find us. That's how they are. Getting water from you would mean to go back *that* way." He cocked his head to the east. Star stared off into the wasteland. All she saw were rocks and a few hills. But it was true; somewhere beyond that landscape was a band of merciless raiders who wanted nothing more than to kill them.

Graf rapidly sucked in several deep breaths, then stood up.

"That syringe…I know what that is! It's medicine, isn't it?!" he said.

"Not yours," Pearce said. "Even if it was, the needle's broken."

"Then we find a new one!" Graf said.

"I will, but not for him," Pearce said.

"You're sick?" Star asked.

"Nothing that'll kill me, so long as I have this." Pearce nudged his pack.

"What are you doing all the way out here with medicine?" Graf felt a rush of realization. The answer came to him the moment he asked. "It can't be…you found the rare Red Flower that can cure any illness?"

"That's what's in that syringe?" Star said.

"Sir…uh, PEARCE!" Graf said, "I'm willing to trade anything. Everything! For that medicine. My son needs it!"

"*I* need it," Pearce said.

"If there's one, we can find another one," Star said.

"Sounds like you have a plan. Good luck," Pearce said.

"Wait," Graf pleaded. "How far along is your illness?"

"It's the Blood Virus," Pearce said. "Whenever it chooses to finish me off."

"It won't be within the next day," Graf said. "I'm BEGGING you. My son doesn't have long. That's why we trekked through this valley to get help, because it was the most direct way. We can get a new syringe, give him the drug, and help you find another flower to heal yourself. You have time, Pearce."

"You have any idea how long it took me to find this thing?" Pearce said, his voice gravelly as he restrained his anger. "As you can see, there's no vegetation here. I've searched all over this valley, and THIS was the only one I found."

Graf stayed back, noticing that the loner's hand was resting on his revolver. The message was clear: he was NOT going to relinquish the medicine.

"There's more," Star said. It was meant to comfort Graf and Paul than anything else. The truth was, she wasn't sure if they could find any in time.

Suddenly, a loud *pop* drew their attention to the southeast. High in the air was a small, fiery explosion. Black smoke trailed from the circle as sparks sizzled out.

"A flare," Star said. They heard the roar of an engine and the scraping of rubber. Her heart raced again as she looked back to the hills, seeing the buggy racing in their direction.

CHAPTER 18

"That didn't take long at all!" Europe said, throwing a fist up enthusiastically. He pulled his goggles over his eye and rotated the flamethrower to aim at the targets.

"Shouldn't we wait for Cedoz to see the flare and join us?" the driver asked.

"Wait? No. I'm not giving this guy a chance to come up with another special plan of escape. No, go right on in! Floor it! We're gonna have ourselves a barbeque!"

"As you wish," the driver said. He pressed his foot to the accelerator. The engine rumbled, shaking the entire buggy as they raced toward their victims. Europe tested the flamethrower again, then waited to be brought close enough. He rested his finger on the trigger, eager to torch the warrior.

Suddenly, several bullets struck the buggy, causing the driver to veer to the left.

"Oh, shit!" he yelled. The buggy passed over a small hill, momentarily going airborne. It bounced upon impact, then fishtailed a full one-eighty degrees before the driver steadied it.

"That was the kid! The fucking KID!" the passenger said.

"Move it!" Europe yelled. "We'll torch him too!"

Paul sat upright, following the buggy with his rifle barrel. At first, he thought he hit the driver, only to realize the truth once the vehicle started rolling again.

He coughed repeatedly. Shaky hands gripped the rifle as he tried to aim once again for the buggy.

"Paul!" Graf said. He ran to his son and helped him up. The vehicle had readjusted and was speeding in their direction, kicking up dirt the entire way. Paul shoved his father away and aimed his rifle again. He fired several shots until his magazine went dry. Most of his bullets went wide, the others crunching against the front of the hull. "Come on, son!" Graf said. He grabbed Paul and threw him over his shoulder, then ran as fast as he could.

The buggy passed by, the driver cursing after failing to run down the targets. He swerved to the left, hoping to catch Star and Pearce. The woman dove out of the way, leaving only the warrior standing a few yards back.

"He's mine!" Europe said. He aimed the flamethrower as the driver slowed down to grant him his glory. A rifle shot struck the nozzle of the flamethrower, jolting the weapon to the left as Europe squeezed the trigger. "Fuck!" he yelled.

The driver floored the pedal again, directing the vehicle at Pearce. Before he closed the distance, he heard gunshots cracking the air in rapid succession. He jolted in place as numerous bullets carved his chest open. He leaned forward and slumped dead against the wheel, keeping the pedal floored.

Pearce dove out of the way as the buggy raced aimlessly past him.

"Wanderer! I will carve your heart out and show it to you while I burn it!" Europe screamed. The buggy bounced over uneven ground, its dead driver still weighing the accelerator down. The passenger reached over to push him out, only to be thrown back in his own seat due to the violent shifting.

Graf put Paul down, then gripped his shotgun.

"Can you run?" he asked. Paul nodded.

"Okay. GO! Go as fast as you can. Don't look back! I'll be right behind you," he said. Graf glanced back to his sister. She had a pistol drawn and pointed toward the buggy, which was now several hundred yards in the distance. "Come on!"

"What about Pearce?" she said.

"He doesn't want our help," Graf said.

"But..."

"Get outta here," Pearce interrupted. Star hesitated. It felt wrong to leave him alone to face the threat.

"Come on!" Graf said. Star looked back at Pearce, realizing he wasn't going to follow them. Finally, she took off running after her brother and nephew. Graf ran behind his son, guiding him toward the ruins of the town. The rubble would provide enough obstacles to keep the vehicle from having a straight shot at them. They found a large brick wall which stood over fourteen feet high.

"Hide here!" Star said. Paul dove behind it and ejected the empty magazine from his rifle. It was his last one, leaving him with a pistol.

"I swear buddy, once we get out of here, you'll never have to shoot a gun again," Graf said.

"In this world?" Star said. "I wouldn't count on it."

The buggy bounced hard then teetered to the left after hitting a pile of rubble.

"Damn it!" Europe yelled. He grabbed the flamethrower mount and held tight to keep himself from falling off. "Will you get him off of that seat?!"

The passenger balanced himself, took a breath, then threw himself over the driver. He reached the door handle and pushed his dead companion out. They heard a *thud* as he hit the dirt, immediately followed by the cracking of bones as the rear tire passed over him. Immediately, the buggy began to slow.

The passenger scooted into the driver's seat and eased on the brake to steady the vehicle further. He turned the vehicle around then glanced back at Europe.

"Keep it going!" Europe said, ripping off the goggles and throwing them to the ground. "Let's get him!"

The raider floored the pedal, billowing clouds of dust from under the tires.

Pearce remained still as the raiders approached. He shouldered his rifle and waited until it was within three hundred feet. After a few short seconds, he could see the crusted face of the driver. With the weapon on full-auto, he aimed for his head and squeezed the trigger.

Only two rounds escaped the muzzle before the weapon jammed. Alarmed, Pearce looked at the cocking lever, which was stuck halfway. He could smell the heat from the buggy's engine as it neared within ten feet.

He dove to his right and somersaulted, the buggy passing less than a foot behind him. He rolled to his feet, heard the hissing of the flamethrower nozzle, then ran as fast as he could.

Europe fired the flamethrower, sending a river of fire scorching the ground. The flame streaked past Pearce as he ran, the speeding buggy inadvertently causing his shot to miss as it sped by.

The loner kept running, his shirt sleeve trailing smoke as it burned.

"You incompetent clown!" Europe yelled at his driver. "Just circle him! Give him no escape!"

Pearce ripped his burning shirt sleeve free and tossed it aside. The skin over his bicep was mildly burnt but was otherwise okay. He returned his attention to the buggy as the driver turned the vehicle in a wide arch. It weaved between a few brick structures, then sped toward him as it escaped the edge of the community remnants.

He pulled his remaining stick of dynamite free and pulled most of the fuse away, leaving an inch remaining. He lit the tip and hurled it like a grenade toward the buggy.

The driver shrieked as he recognized the flares from a burning dynamite fuse coming straight at him. He veered sharply to the left and floored the accelerator. The dynamite exploded, causing the buggy to shake violently.

Europe was thrown from the mount, tucking his head down as he hit the ground. He rolled like a barrel for several yards while the vehicle continued speeding off without him.

Fighting for control, the driver veered back to the right, taking the buggy in a tight circle. At that moment, he located Pearce with his eyes. Feeling the urge to run him down again, he pushed the buggy to its maximum speed, kicking a trail of dust behind him.

With his rifle jammed and his dynamite used up, Pearce was down to his revolver. He drew the weapon and aimed for the driver. The buggy rocked and bounced over the uneven ground, making it difficult to line up a shot. He fired once, missing wide. The next shot punched through the hood. The buggy was coming in fast, the raider baring teeth with a sadistic laugh. Pearce fired the remaining four shots.

The laugh turned into a pained cry as one of those bullets hit right by his head, shredding his ear. He jolted in his seat, accidentally turning the wheel to the right. Pearce moved in the opposite direction, steering clear of the buggy. The raider continued racing off, eventually turning in a wide circle.

He watched it carefully as he grabbed another speed-loader. This was his last of two, though he had a few .38 caliber rounds tucked in his vest. He filled the cylinder and waited for the buggy to make another move toward him.

It was that moment when he heard running steps coming at him.

Pearce turned and saw Europe charging.

"I'm gonna kill you!" he yelled, closing within a couple yards. He unwrapped the chain from his vest and drew it back. Pearce rotated his body and pointed the weapon. The chain lashed like a whip, striking the frame of the weapon. Pearce stumbled back, feeling the gun knocked from his grip.

Europe advanced, whipping the chain wildly. There was no rhythm to his movements; he simply thrashed the chain whichever way he pleased.

Pearce continued to backtrack, waiting for the attacker to make a move. Europe smiled ear-to-ear. His eye sparkled as he envisioned the many ways he wanted to kill the warrior.

Finally, he whipped the chain at Pearce's head. It struck nothing but air as he ducked. Europe lashed again. Pearce ducked again, allowing the chain to pass harmlessly above him. Frustrated, Europe slashed at an angle.

This time, the chain struck, lashing Pearce's right shoulder. The loner gritted his teeth in pain, then lunged forward.

Europe lashed with the other end of the chain. Pearce threw his hands up. The chain struck right above the wrists, causing his hands to retract out of pain. Europe swung the long end of the chain. It landed on the back of Pearce's neck and wrapped around like a snake.

Pearce felt his airway close off as Europe yanked back on the chain, drawing him closer. He slashed the short end, slicing Pearce near the temple. His head snapped back from the impact as blood trickled down his face.

"The look suits you," Europe said, drawing his arm back for another swing. Pearce snapped a kick into his abdomen. Spit and air exploded from Europe's mouth as his gut caved in. Pearce grabbed the chain and pulled it back, hyperextending Europe's reach, then thrust another kick into his ribs. Europe gasped and fell backward, still hanging on to the chain.

Pearce unwrapped it from around his neck and advanced on the raider. Europe stood up and swung the chain in a wide arch. Pearce held up a fist, blocking the swing. The chain wrapped repeatedly around his forearm and wrist, all the way up to his hand which clenched around the end. Pearce moved in, first hitting Europe in the face with a left jab, then with a right hook from his chained arm.

The metal links scraped Europe's jaw as the blow passed over his face. Pearce swung his arm back, catching the thug near his eye. Europe staggered backwards. With both hands, he yanked the chain back, freeing it from Pearce's arm.

He snarled like an enraged beast and slashed the chain repeatedly. Pearce evaded the first three strikes by backing out of range. Europe continued advancing, persistently swinging the weapon high and low. Finally, he swung with all his might, the chain passing just shy of his enemy's face.

Pearce moved in and threw another kick, driving his heel into Europe's chest and launching him backward. He pulled his knife and advanced, ready to bring the clash to a dead end.

His ears picked up the sound of racing tires and a roaring engine, rapidly growing louder. Pearce glanced over his shoulder and saw the buggy racing right for him. The buggy struck as he dove to his left, colliding with his leg. He spun like a wheel in midair, losing the knife somewhere in the process, before hitting the ground, kicking up dirt like splashing water.

The nerves in his left leg flared up, causing him to tense. Something in his thigh was cracked.

He could hear the vehicle turning several yards away, preparing to make another go at him. Ignoring the pain, Pearce pushed himself to his feet.

Europe charged him from behind and slashed with the chain, striking him in the back of the head. Pearce staggered forward, limping on his left leg. He turned around, his vision hazy. Europe slashed again, the chain striking down near his collarbone.

Pearce sprang and plowed a left fist into his jaw, driving him back. He punched again, splitting his lip. Europe, spitting blood, advanced with another slash of the chain. Pearce leaned to the left and tucked his head, narrowly dodging the swing. He snapped his right leg up and around, connecting the top of his foot into Europe's stomach.

Europe jolted backward from the devastating blow, causing him to fall to one knee. Pearce moved in and threw another punch into his temple. Spit and teeth spewed onto the dirt as Europe faceplanted.

He heard the buggy coming again. Pearce looked, saw it nearing within a few meters, then dove out of the way. He cleared its path by less than a foot, the buggy nearly running Europe over as it passed by.

Pearce's leg was throbbing nonstop as he stood up. He straightened his posture and watched the buggy as it circled. The driver would be making another go at him in a few moments.

Peeking around the edge of the brick wall, Paul's body tensed as he watched Pearce evade the buggy a third time by diving out of the way. He had watched the entire conflict and flinched when he witnessed Pearce get hit by the buggy. He could tell the man was hurt by the way he walked.

The buggy was circling again, ready to try a fourth time in a row. Pearce was clearly in pain and growing fatigued.

"Oh, God," Star said. "I don't know how much longer he can last."

"There isn't much we can do," Graf said. "We have to move. The rest of the gang are following that flare. They're coming here as we speak."

Paul checked his pistol, then watched as the buggy circled. Pearce and the one-eyed bandit engaged in another clash. The raider struck low with the chain, hitting Pearce in the injured leg. The one-eyed man ran back as the buggy made its run at the loner, who barely managed to get out of the way. The buggy continued forward for several meters. Paul saw the wheels turn to the left as it slowed, prepping for a turn.

He chambered a round in his pistol and ran forward. Graf and Star stood up, alarmed. Graf reached for his son but missed.

"Paul! What are you doing?! Get back here!"

The boy ignored his father and ran at the buggy. It continued to turn, unintentionally lining up with him. He could see the driver through the empty windshield, his neck and vest covered in blood.

Paul aimed his pistol and fired repeatedly. The raider arched back in his seat as a dozen rounds penetrated his chest.

Europe looked to the sound of gunfire. The buggy rolled to a stop, the driver leaning dead against the steering wheel. Several feet ahead of it stood the boy. He held a pistol in hand, the slide locked back.

"You little bastard!" Europe yelled.

Thirty feet away, Pearce pushed himself up, his leg throbbing intensely. He glanced to the buggy, seeing the driver dead and the boy standing in front of it. He then saw Europe whirling his chain while advancing on the kid.

Pearce stood up and sprinted, only making a few steps before succumbing to the pain in his leg and falling to his knees. Breathing heavily, he grabbed a softball-sized rock. He stood back up, took careful aim, then threw the rock.

It struck Europe behind the ear, causing him to stumble to his right. He whipped himself around, his face like a crazed one-eyed lunatic. He twirled the chain, then charged.

Pearce raised his fists and waited for the raider to close the distance. The chain sliced the air, missing its target. Europe swung back, again missing. Breathing heavily, he lunged for a heavier strike. Pearce sprang and reached out, catching his arm mid-swing.

Europe's head snapped back as Pearce threw an elbow into his nose, then with the same arm, punched him in the stomach twice. With both hands, Pearce twisted Europe's arm clockwise, prying the chain loose from his grasp and tossed it aside. A knee to the face sent Europe stumbling backward.

Bleeding from the nose and mouth, the raider closed his fist and rushed the warrior, only to catch a jab to the nose. Pearce struck again, this time to the ribs, then a right hook to the jaw. Europe stumbled back, teetering on his heels. His eye patch dangled from his face, exposing a red scab where his eye was.

Pearce rotated to the right, bringing his leg high in an arching motion. The heel crashed onto Europe's temple, causing him to spin repeatedly before hitting the ground.

Pearce hobbled back on his good leg, taking a moment to adjust to the pain. On the ground nearby was the chain. He picked it up then advanced. Europe was gradually pushing himself up off the ground when he felt the chain thrown around his neck. He gagged as it tightened. Pearce rotated his hips and pulled upward, bringing Europe off his feet. Like holding a potato sack, he let the raider hang over his shoulder, kicking his feet until he suffocated.

Finally, the body went limp. Pearce dropped him and stepped away. He glanced back at the buggy, confirming to himself that the third raider was dead. As he looked, his eyes went to Paul, who stared back at him.

Pearce was not good with 'thank yous', especially when it came to people whom he wanted nothing to do with.

That's practically everybody, his mind added. Wasting no time, he began searching for his revolver.

He would need it.

CHAPTER 19

The wind brushed through Lassa's hair as she scanned the horizon with her binoculars. She was in the passenger seat of Cedoz's semi-truck, her lord having taken the wheel himself.

The flare was less than a thousand yards directly ahead, its smoky trail descending down past a few hills.

"I don't see Europe anywhere," she said. "He must be beyond those hills."

"The damn fool. He took it upon himself to catch those people," Cedoz said. Behind his calm voice and demeanor, Lassa could sense a storm brewing within him. She had been at his side for many years and had seen many raids and clashes with other gangs. They had lost people before, but they always paved the way to victory. This time, however? Cedoz had never lost so many people, especially not to such a small group.

"We will make them pay the price," Cedoz said.

"We have lost many, my lord," she said. Cedoz could sense the apprehension in her voice. The feeling was spreading throughout the entire group. They needed motivation; a reminder of what they were doing.

"ALL STOP!" he commanded. Lassa stood and raised a fist, signaling to the group as he hit the brakes. The buggies and trucks hit their brakes as they gathered around Cedoz's semi-truck. He stood up on the seat, making sure he could be seen by all of his people.

"You're wondering why we continue, after everything we've been through," he said to them. "I can see it in your eyes. You saw what this stranger can do to us. One man. You may be asking, 'Is the act of revenge worthy of such a cost?'"

"We serve you, Cedoz," one of the raiders called out. "We will pay the cost in blood."

"Yet, I sense fear in your voice," Cedoz said. "But not fear of the warrior; fear of *me*. You are afraid to speak your minds because you know it is not wise to be disloyal. You pursue this man because of me. Now, let me remind you why catching these travelers is good for *you*."

"The water!" Lassa yelled out.

"The sacrifice of our people will not be for naught. We will find their community and seize their resources; their water. Whoever has water, has power in this land. Any man can go for days without food. But the strongest man can't last a day in this sun without water. These travelers, whoever they are, they carried more water in their travels than we've seen in a month. Wherever they came from, there's more. And we will find it. But…I need your help."

The group cheered, raising their weapons high. Others revved their engines. Others clanged swords together, symbolizing an undying allegiance to their leader.

Satisfied that morale had been restored, Cedoz took his seat and slammed his foot against the accelerator. The truck raced ahead, followed by his band of raiders in their fanatic crusade.

****

"Paul!" Graf said, embracing his son. "Boy, you could've gotten yourself killed." Paul shook his head in protest then pointed at Pearce. Graf looked, seeing the loner holstering his revolver. He walked with a limp, bleeding from his hands and face as he searched for his pack. Graf sighed, thinking of his inaction behind the wall while Pearce fought the bandits. It was Paul, a nine-year-old boy, who selflessly raced out to help someone; someone who refused to help, no less. It was only by circumstance that Pearce had defended them against the raiders. Yet, Paul didn't care. He simply did what was right. Graf looked back at his son. "How did you ever get to be so brave?"

Paul smiled weakly, then took a seat in the buggy. Star pulled the dead bandit from the driver's seat then tested the engine.

"It seems okay!" she said. "We can use this."

"We're gonna need to," Graf said, looking up at the residue from the flare. "We've got to go." He briefly inspected the engine to see if there was any damage. Luckily, the mechanisms were left undamaged from the shootout. "Okay. Paul, get in." Paul climbed into the backseat, looking back at Pearce the entire time. Graf sighed, then climbed into the passenger seat. "Drive up to him," he told Star.

Pearce was leaning heavily on his right leg as he picked up his pack. His face was caked with dust that had mixed with sweat. His sleeveless arm had been scorched, and he bled from various gashes on his head and hands.

"Hey!" Graf said as Star pulled the buggy alongside him. "Get in."

"You're better off going your own way," Pearce said.

"Oh, stop with that loner shit," Graf said. "Look at you! You're a mess! The rest of those maniacs will be here any second. What's your grand plan? Hobble away on one leg? If so, mind lending us that Red Flower? Because you're not gonna survive what's coming."

Pearce glared at him angrily. Who was he to give lectures on survival? Had it not been for this family crossing paths with him, Pearce would be on his way out of Tidal Valley, heading to less hostile territory.

His gaze went past Graf and into the hills. Dust was swirling in huge clouds. Out of those clouds came a convoy of vehicles. In the lead was the semi with no top, carrying Cedoz. Behind it were seven buggies, plus an eighth that had a mounted machine gun on it, along with five pickup trucks, and over a dozen motorcycles.

Pearce grabbed his pack and climbed into the back, taking position with the flamethrower.

"You know how to drive?" he said to Star.

"It's been a while," she said.

Great, Pearce thought. He tested the nozzle, sparking a small flame. Star hit the accelerator, rocking the buggy as she raced east.

He watched as the army of raiders closed in. The motorcycles jumped high from speeding over the hills, reminding him of a pod of dolphins looping over an ocean surface. Faster and more adept to the terrain, they easily outmatched the buggy in speed and maneuverability.

Each driver carried a pistol of some kind. Considering how well they drove the bikes, Pearce had no doubt that they would struggle shooting while operating the bikes.

"Shit, we're not gonna outrun them," Graf said.

"We have no choice," Star said. Pearce kept the nozzle pointed out, sending small streams of flame to warn the gang back. They ignored the threat and kept pace barely out of range at fifty feet. Several of them began to break away, forming a large pincer that gradually encircled their buggy.

"Turn around," Pearce said. Star looked back at him, then at the trucks behind the motorcycles, which gradually drew closer.

"Turn around? Attack?"

"It's the only thing that'll work," Pearce said.

"Oh, God," Graf muttered. He calmed himself and carefully studied the situation. Pearce had a point. Either they turn around and engage, thus risking being captured or killed; or keep retreating until they ran out of fuel, in which case, they'd certainly be captured or killed. "DO IT!"

Star hit the brakes and cut the wheel. The buggy rotated like a top until its engine was pointed directly behind them. With its sudden stop, the motorcycles behind it rapidly drew closer…

Right within range of the flamethrower.

Pearce squeezed the trigger. Like a dragon from ancient times, the nozzle spit an orange river of flame. The motorcycles broke formation, but not before two of them were engulfed in fire. They overturned, their drivers screaming in agony as the fire ate at their flesh. The fire stuck like sap, clinging to their clothes and skin, burning all to a crisp.

Star floored the pedal, speeding directly at the semi. Pearce rotated the turret, scorching the ground behind them as he swept the fire at the other bikers. They separated into two groups, going left and right out of range. Star and Graf tensed as they rapidly approached the convoy. Directly ahead was the semi. It drove directly toward them, its path never wavering to avoid a crash.

"Keep going," Pearce said.

Star was shaking now. They could see the mask worn by the leader through the empty windshield.

Cedoz gazed back at them. They were driving in Europe's vehicle. That was three more of his Dirt Diamonds whose lives were claimed by the warrior, plus two of his bikers. He kept moving, aligning himself with the buggy.

"You think you're brave," he muttered, speeding toward them.

"A buggy vs. a semi? They won't survive the crash," Lassa warned.

"That may not be true. I'm sure at least ONE will live long enough to tell us what we need," he said. He put all of his weight on the pedal, putting the truck at top speed.

Star was starting to hyperventilate.

The distance closed within a few short seconds. Five hundred feet.

Four hundred…three…two…

One hundred feet…

Pearce aimed the nozzle directly ahead. By the time he aimed, they were fifty feet within collision.

Finally, he unleashed a stream of flame. Cedoz cut the wheel hard to the right. In doing so, he smashed into a buggy traveling parallel to it. It flipped over repeatedly before smashing into a boulder, crushing all four of its occupants. The semi spun out of control, its driver's side doused in flame.

Pearce kept the stream going, scorching two of the buggies as well as a semi. The convoy broke apart, as though the buggy was a flaming meteorite coursing through the galaxy.

Cedoz eased on the brakes, slowing the truck until he regained control.

"Get after them!" he yelled. "Shoot for the driver. The tires. Anything. Use the RPGs!"

The gang circled back, passing the burning buggies and its dying occupants as they gave chase. Raiders in the rear and passenger seats aimed their rifles and fired at the enemy vehicle.

Pearce crouched, hearing the bullets whistle by his head. The Dirt Diamonds were closing in, positioning themselves to encircle the buggy once more. The nearest ones were smart enough to keep out of range of his flamethrower. Another bullet struck nearby.

"Keep your head down," Graf said to Paul. The boy leaned down as far as he could, while his father took the pistol and aimed back at the trucks. Another round struck the side, skidding just above the tire and past his head. "Shit!" he exclaimed. He checked himself briefly for injuries, then took aim.

His mind flashed back to a moment three years prior. He and Paul had gone out to check on their windmill with a third companion, when two men rode up to them on horseback. They didn't waste time making their intentions known: they simply wanted to rob and kill. Graf was the faster draw that day, but the guilt of taking another life haunted him.

But now, that guilt had dissipated. Now, he had witnessed the evil that lurked in this world. He knew that sheltering his son, or himself, from the wicked in this world was impossible. This was the lesson he had to learn.

Graf lined his eye with the iron sights, placing the buggy driver in the center notch. It was over a hundred feet away, driving fifty miles per hour on rough ground. He followed its path and fired. The first bullet struck low, hitting the hood. The next was higher, but wide, hitting the side bar of the windshield frame. He fired again, this time hitting the driver directly in the heart.

The buggy veered sharply to the right, much to the dismay of its passengers. They clamored over the driver in a vain attempt to grab the wheel. Racing at top speed, it smashed into a half-buried piece of debris. The engine crumpled inward, crushing the passenger, while flinging the other two high into the air.

Star shrieked as several more bullets struck near her. She lurched backward as one sparked against the wheel, skidding out through the windshield. She glanced left, seeing two of the pickup trucks traveling parallel with them. Behind them was another buggy, keeping a distance of a hundred feet to keep out of range of the flamethrower.

Pearce watched them, while keeping an eye on the several bikers that pursued directly behind. A barrage of bullets struck near, a couple hitting the turret, millimeters from his flesh.

"Hit the brakes!" he yelled to Star. Following his instructions, she brought the buggy to a screeching stop. At the same time, he fired off the flamethrower, dousing the bikers in flame as they unwittingly sped within range.

Three bikes flipped and smashed into the dirt, while their drivers rolled on the ground in agony.

Star stomped her foot on the accelerator, bringing the buggy back to full speed. She looked ahead and screamed as the trucks had circled around, bringing themselves on a collision course with her. She swerved to the right, narrowly avoiding the first. The second adjusted its path and cut hard to its left, striking the buggy near the rear.

The impact shook the vehicle, throwing Pearce to the side. Holding on to the turret rail, he hung over the side of the Jeep. The truck that missed adjusted its path and lined itself along the buggy's passenger side. Two raiders emerged from the window, their pistols aimed at Pearce.

Bullets struck near the windshield, nicking the driver.

Graf fired his pistol, emptying the magazine as the truck veered away. He continued squeezing the trigger, hearing multiple clicks before he realized the mag was spent.

"Damn it, I'm out," he said. All that remained now was the shotgun.

Pearce pulled himself back up onto the turret, then fired a hot stream along the ground. Fire swirled in a thin trail, forcing the numerous vehicles to swerve to avoid getting scorched.

A bullet struck the nozzle, bursting the metal shaft into pieces. Pearce leaned back, realizing the M60 had opened fire on them. Several more bullets struck along the side of the buggy, striking the rear left tire. Shreds of rubber flopped onto the ground as the wheel continued to rotate, causing the buggy to drag to the left. Several more shots bombarded the vehicle. Pearce groaned in pain as one nicked him in the side, cracking a rib. He fell to his knees and drew his revolver. Aiming slightly ahead of the driver, he fired all six cylinders.

The driver and passenger pitched in their seats as the bullets came in through the window, hitting them each in the chest. The gunner fired rapidly, his aim going wide as the dead driver leaned on the wheel, steering the buggy deep into the valley.

Star gritted her teeth and veered to the right, trying to regain control. The buggy vibrated as it continued on, slowing to forty miles per hour.

"Look out!" Graf yelled. Star looked to the right, realizing she was steering them toward the edge of a cliff.

"Holy—" she jerked the wheel to the left. The buggy swerved, its passenger tires brushing the rocky ledge as she straightened their path. She traveled along the ledge for several hundred feet, then gradually steered to the left to generate distance.

The valley below the cliff was vast and empty. The drop itself was at least two hundred feet, the ground directly below lined with edged rocks that could bludgeon a man's skull.

Falling would result in a bloody mess.

The motorcycles accelerated, their drivers aiming pistols at Pearce. With the flamethrower out of commission, Pearce took cover behind the turret. The bikers opened fire, while one of the buggies sped up twenty feet alongside Star. The raiders in the front and back passenger seats aimed their rifles at Star. She gasped and hit the brakes, throwing off their aim as they sped up ahead of them. They jerked their aim to the right and popped off several rounds, peppering the engine and door.

Star yelped as one of the rounds pierced her shoulder, causing her to arch backward in pain.

"Star!" Graf yelled. He opened his door and leaned out, aiming his shotgun at the gunners. The scatter shot was useless at this range, the pellets flying wide of his intended target.

The shooters continued firing, hitting Graf in the arm and hip.

"AGH!" he yelled, losing the shotgun. More shots whizzed by as he forced himself back into the vehicle.

Star pressed a hand to her shoulder as blood poured down over her chest and arm.

"They've got us boxed in," she said.

"We can't give up," Graf said. He groaned in pain as he looked back to check on his son. "Paul! You hurt?"

The boy responded with a thumbs up. Graf forced a smile, which disappeared as he gazed back. The pursuing trucks and buggies broke off to the side, making way for the semi.

"Son of a bitch…Star? Go faster," he said. She glanced back, seeing the vehicle rapidly closing in. She tried veering left, only to be sideswiped by one of the trucks. They were trapped.

Cedoz gunned the accelerator. Like a giant bullet, he rammed the buggy, causing it to pitch forward. It began to fishtail, its rear tires scraping the edge of the cliff. Cedoz backed off, realizing his plan was about to backfire.

Lassa stood up and leaned through the empty windshield frame. The gang looked back, seeing her swaying a hand to the left. They understood the instruction: make space.

Star steered to the left as well. There was no choice. Twice now, they had nearly gone over the cliff.

Cedoz rammed them again, jolting all three passengers in their seats. He eased back in preparation for another shot.

"You got to go left," Graf said. "Plow right through them!"

"It won't work," Star said. "They won't let up."

"Let him get close again," Pearce said. Graf looked back at him.

"What? Why?"

Pearce answered with a glare. "What did I say about questioning my instructions?"

Graf nodded. "Good point."

Pearce moved around the turret rail, keeping a crouched position as he moved around the bed of the buggy.

Cedoz floored the pedal, bringing the semi in for the kill. Pearce leaned forward and waited. The truck made contact.

Pearce leapt forward, landing on the hood of the truck. He dropped into a slide, putting his heel right in Cedoz's face. Leaning up on his elbow, Pearce kicked the warlord in the nose, snapping his head back. He kicked again, this time putting his heel into his eye socket.

The semi slowed, giving the family the ability to make some distance.

Lassa stood up and pulled the shotgun that rested between her and Cedoz, then thrust it into Pearce's chest.

He grabbed the barrel and thrust it skyward. Both barrels discharged into the air.

The loner propped himself on his knees as the woman grabbed a knife. Shrieking madly, she thrust the blade to his neck. The battle cry turned into a scream as Pearce grabbed her wrist and twisted it clockwise, locking her hand up. A second twisting jolt shook the knife from her hand, sending it bouncing off the hood.

Without skipping a beat, Pearce grabbed her by the hair and yanked her close, then slammed an elbow into her face. He struck again, and saw Cedoz reaching for something below the dashboard. He kicked the leader in the eye, knocking him back in the seat, then rammed a fist into Lassa's nose, knocking her back as well.

He looked back, seeing a group of bikers drawing near. They had their pistols aimed, though they couldn't risk firing without hitting Cedoz or Lassa.

Pearce reached in and grabbed the steering wheel, then veered the truck sharply to the left. The truck bumped as it plowed into the group, grinding metal and bodies into the soil beneath it.

Cedoz lunged and grabbed Pearce by the throat. Pearce released the wheel and tried to free himself from the leader's grip. The fingers closed over his airway like kraken tentacles crushing a ship. Pearce grabbed at his wrists but could not outmuscle the leader's grasp.

He snapped a punch into Cedoz's face, striking near the eye. He struck repeatedly, drawing blood. Yet, the leader maintained his grip. Pearce could feel his energy waning.

Lassa smiled at him, her face bruised and bleeding.

"First, we're gonna kill you! Then we're going to kill them!" she said, nodding her head back at the family. "Rest assured; their deaths will be slow and tedious. And the woman, well…she'll have it the worst." That smile widened. "Then again, maybe the boy—"

Pearce reached in and grabbed the wheel, then veered the truck sharply to the right. Lassa smiled, the momentum throwing her into the back of her seat. Her eyes went wide as she saw the cliff come into view directly ahead. The sudden maneuver loosened the leader's grip, allowing Pearce to leap over the side. He hit the ground and rolled over his shoulder as the truck raced to the ledge.

Cedoz hit the brakes, but it was too late. Survival was the sole objective. He dove out the door and hit the ground, setting right at the ledge. Lassa, however, was not fast enough to act.

The truck soared off the cliff edge and arched down. Lassa sucked in a breath as she watched the rocky floor grow closer and closer. The truck smashed down engine-first, caving into the seats. A brief shriek left her lungs before being crushed by a tidal wave of rock and metal.

Star could hear the explosion behind her but didn't look back. The convoy kept pace, continuing to fire a few rounds at their tires. Now, the front left wheel was flat, causing the buggy to drag.

She veered left in an attempt to sideswipe one of the trucks, but it easily outmaneuvered her. Another pickup circled to their right, lined itself up, and accelerated to top speed. It struck the passenger side, flipping the buggy over its top.

Pearce stood up then turned to the sound of the crash. He saw the buggy flip, the Dirt Diamonds circling it like hungry sharks. The surviving bikers regrouped and sped toward him. Pearce drew his revolver and fired, hitting one of them in the chest. The others broke formation and started a wide circle.

It was then that Pearce realized they were staring past him. He turned around and pointed his gun at the charging Cedoz.

The leader swung a fist, knocking the gun from his grasp.

"He's mine!" he warned the bikers. Pearce backed up, unable to hide his limp. Cedoz advanced, hands open to grab and strangle him.

Pearce faked a punch to the head, tricking Cedoz's hands to guard high, then kicked him in the ribs. Cedoz snarled, the force driving him back a few steps. Pearce advanced and struck him in the face with a right hook, then a left. A third punch was stopped prematurely, the fist landing square in Cedoz's palm. Pearce lunged with his left fist, only to have the same result.

Cedoz looked him in the eye. *My turn.*

He thrust a kick down on Pearce's injured leg, flaring the pain like wildfire. The leader pressed the attack with a series of punches to the face and ribs, each blow a staggering one. Another kick to the leg dropped Pearce to his hands and knees, and a devastating kick to the ribs rolled him to his back.

Cedoz waited, savoring the kill as he allowed Pearce to recover.

Bleeding from the nose, temple, and mouth, Pearce stood up and threw a punch, which the leader easily evaded. Cedoz countered with a kick to the stomach before grabbing him again by the throat. Pearce felt his throat close, cutting off his airway for the second time.

The leader was bigger and stronger. His grip would not be pried by brute force, but by body mechanics. Pearce raised an arm high over his head, then drove his elbow down over Cedoz's arms, forcing them to bend at the elbows. Pearce ducked and turned, slipping free from the hold.

He struck a blow to the mask. Cedoz suddenly lurched back, this time displaying a true sense of pain. The blow had slipped the mask to the side, revealing the rotten flesh that had eaten away his jaw. Contact with the air triggered the nerves, forcing him to fix the mask. Pearce struck another blow to the face, driving Cedoz back further, then drove a kick high into his chest.

Pearce's entire thigh was throbbing by now. The pain had intensified to the point where he could barely put any weight on it. Despite this, he advanced, though slower than he intended.

Cedoz repositioned the mask then charged. Pearce threw a punch, which was detected by a circular block. He threw another punch, only to have his arm caught in the leader's hands, then twisted and locked. A knee to the abdomen doubled him over. A moment later, that same knee struck him in the face. A blow to the temple knocked him back to the ground.

The world was spinning around him as Pearce struggled to get to his feet. Cedoz stood over him.

"I admire your persistence. Unfortunately for you, it wasn't enough," he said. He stomped a foot down on Pearce's spine, pinning him down. "As Lassa said, you will be the first to die. Then the boy and his father, and slowly. The woman will be saved for last. And considering the price that we've paid, thanks to you, it may be a long drawn out experience for her."

"Go ahead. Like I give a shit," Pearce grumbled, spitting dirt.

"You wanna pretend you don't care? That's fine, but don't expect that trick to work on me," Cedoz said. Pearce tried to push up, only for Cedoz to press down harder with his foot. He glanced around, seeing several Raiders standing nearby. Thirty feet directly ahead was the cliff edge.

"Then again, who cares?" Cedoz continued. He grabbed Pearce by the vest and lifted him up. His bikers moved in, drawing knives to carve him up in a ritual fashion. "You're gonna die anyway. I guess you'll have to watch from Hell."

"Yeah, speaking of Hell," Pearce mumbled. Cedoz felt a hot flame brush against his midsection. He looked down, seeing Paul's lighter ignited in Pearce's hand as it scorched the fuse on the pack of dynamite he wore on his belt.

Cedoz dropped his opponent and quickly scrambled to rip the explosive free. Pearce turned around and ran for the cliff. One of the raiders attempted to obstruct him, only to be knocked down by an elbow to the face. Despite the limp, Pearce quickly reached the edge of the cliff. He darted left, running along the edge as raiders fired shots at him. The path took him to a pointed jagged peak of land that extended from the ledge like a giant tooth.

Cedoz ripped the pack of dynamite free. There was only a couple seconds' worth of fuse left.

Taking aim at the warrior, he launched it toward the cliff. Pearce covered his head and ducked as the explosive struck a dozen feet away. The fuse burnt away, triggering the nitroglycerin.

The explosion rocked the cliff edge, causing chunks of debris to rain down. Pearce hit the ground, then felt a sudden weightlessness as the entire shelf crumbled beneath him. A tornado of dust consumed him as he rode the avalanche down to the bottom of the cliff.

The raiders pulled the family free from under the buggy and immediately tied their wrists together with rope. Star rocked on her feet, on the verge of passing out. She saw the band of raiders gathering around. Several yards to the west was the cloud of dust where Pearce had fallen.

"Oh, God," Star said, realizing what happened.

Graf struggled against his captors, only to be floored by a punch to the stomach.

"Just let my boy go," he pleaded.

Cedoz stepped alongside Paul, who was down on his hands and knees. He saw the signs of infection near his neck as well as his pale complexion.

"Now why would I do that?" Cedoz taunted.

"Come on," Graf said. "He's a kid! He didn't do anything."

"By the looks of him, anything I do to him might be considered mercy," Cedoz said. He pointed to his band of Dirt Diamonds. "Take them away. No funny business with her," he gestured to Star, "not yet anyway."

"Yes, my lord," the men said. They grabbed their captives and dragged them onto one of the trucks.

"You!" Cedoz said, pointing at two of his bikers. They quickly stepped forward.

"Yes, my lord?"

"Find a way down the cliff. Find me his body," Cedoz said, tilting his head at the dust cloud.

"My lord, he's certainly dead," one of them said.

"Then the job should be easy," Cedoz said. He stepped closer, his chest nearly touching the biker's. "Unless you're not up for the task…"

The raiders stepped back and bowed their heads. "Apologies, my Lord. We will do as you ask."

Cedoz took one last look at the dust cloud, then at his gang of Dirt Diamonds. The warrior had cut his group in half. Had he not killed Boyle, the warrior would have made an excellent lieutenant.

"What a shame," he said to himself. A buggy pulled up alongside him. He took a seat and rested, watching the landscape pass by as the group rode off.

CHAPTER 20

Pearce awoke, lying face down in the dirt at the bottom of the cliff. The air was thick with dust, nearly obscuring the rock wall towering behind him. He coughed, expelling saliva blackened by dirt. His ears still rang from the dynamite blast. For a moment, he wasn't even sure if he was alive. Then, he tried to move, resulting in a spiking pain in his leg.

As fate had it, he rode the top of the ledge all the way to the bottom, preventing him from being crushed by thousands of pounds of dirt and rock. He didn't even remember hitting the bottom.

Clawing the ground with his hands, he pulled himself forward, only to black out again.

The dust cloud could still be seen, even as the bikers drove south where the land sloped around the cliff. Biking down the incline was an easy task, save for a few reptiles that got in the way. They drove along the foot of the cliff and followed it all the way to the cloud.

"What if he's buried under all that rock?" one of them said.

"Then Cedoz will expect us to dig him out," the other said. As they drew near, they could see the enormous pile of earth that had spilled from the shelf. It was as though the dynamite had opened an artery of dirt and rock.

There, at the edge of the spill, was the warrior.

"I'll be damned! He's still alive!"

"We should take his head off ourselves!"

"No, Cedoz will want him for himself."

"Doesn't mean we can't inflict some pain ourselves. Maybe take a hand or a foot off? Rub some sand into the wound?"

His companion thought for a moment. They stepped away from their bikes and stood over Pearce's body.

"Perhaps you have a point," he said. He reached down and grabbed Pearce by the collar, tearing some of the fabric as he lifted him up. He tapped him on the face, stirring him awake. "Hope your nap was nice."

His companion took some sand and rubbed it into the burn on his arm. Pearce shook from the sudden pain, his teeth grinding together.

"You like that? How 'bout this?" the thug said, raising a knee into Pearce's groin. The warrior refused to cry out. The raider continued to hold him up by the collar as the other pulled a large knife.

"Which hand should we take?" he said.

"Hmmm…how 'bout both?!"

His companion laughed. "Sounds good to me. Let's find a good stone to use as a cutting board—"

A gunshot rippled through the air. The thug holding Pearce heard a splattering sound, then the thud of a body falling over. His companion hit the ground, his skull opened up by a rifle bullet. Another shot rang out. The thug yelped as he felt a piercing pain in his leg.

Pearce summoned his energy and lashed his arms out, grabbing the thug by the jaw and hair. With a violent twist, he snapped his neck, dropping both of them back to the ground.

He crawled a few feet away, his vision still hazy. He could hear someone approaching, though his vision was so blurry he couldn't even see. The footsteps were heavy, traveling in a galloping rhythm.

A shadow overtook him. A moment later, Pearce felt himself being lifted off the ground.

He blacked out again.

CHAPTER 21

Pearce awoke, feeling the padding of a bed against his back. He saw four walls and a ceiling. Candles and a lantern lit the room, giving it a minty smell. He sat up quickly, his defensive instincts putting him on alert. The last thing he remembered were the two raiders, the gunfire, and the stranger who approached.

"Whoa!" someone called out. "Take it easy there, traveler! You're alright!"

A man with a long white beard approached and placed a hand on his shoulder. It was then that Pearce realized his burn had been wrapped. "Just rest," the man continued. "You took a hell of a beating, going up against those devils."

Pearce remained seated upright, staring at the man. The beard, the overalls, the cloak, it all looked familiar. It was the old man whose water farm was raided by the Dirt Diamonds. Pearce struggled to subdue his look of surprise. They had decided to let the man live after all.

It seemed plausible. They probably deemed him as a non-threat. Plus, he was able to conjure up water, which they had likely stolen.

The memory of the raid flashed in his mind.

Someone else came in, holding a syringe and what appeared to be an antibiotic. It was a woman, her hair black and knotted behind her head. Her face was bruised, her posture hunched, her dignity taken. There was a stiffness in the way she walked.

Pearce recognized her. Her screams echoed in his memory. Her shirt and pants hid only a few of the bruises she sustained. For the first time in his life, Pearce felt a tightness in his stomach. It wasn't nausea; just some other type of pain he couldn't describe. His mind was like a whirlpool, thinking of the evil event he had witnessed, and did nothing to prevent.

It was obvious that most, if not all, the men had their way with her. There were bruises and bite marks along her neck, all human.

The old man accepted the syringe and meds, then guided his daughter out of the room.

"Go rest, dear," he said. Pearce could see the hurt in his eyes. Behind them was a mental agony, having to witness the horrible things done to his daughter and to his land. The man took a seat by the bed then extended a tray of potatoes. "We have food for you. It's not much but…"

'It's enough," Pearce said. He ate the two potatoes and downed the small cup of water.

"You have a name?" the old man asked.

"Yes," Pearce said. Silence followed. He never liked small talk. He didn't care for talk of any kind, really. He preferred keeping to himself. However, considering what this stranger had done for him, it was the least he could do. "Pearce."

"Nice to meet you, Pearce," the old man said. "I'm Carlos. What are you doing out here in Tidal Rock?"

"Blood virus," he said.

"Oh," Carlos said, nodding his head. "I'm sorry to hear that, young man. I wish I had the medicine to save you. So far, there hasn't been a viable cure."

"I'm aware," Pearce said.

"How far along is it?"

"Enough to be coughing blood."

"I see. Let me help, son. We can provide you food and water and keep you comfortable until…you know."

"Not necessary. I must go. Thanks for the food," Pearce said. He stood up and collected his few remaining items. As he did, he noticed the pain in his leg was very minimal. His thigh was wrapped tightly, nearly cutting off the circulation. He looked back at Carlos. "Did you do something?"

"It's temporary," Carlos said. "Those bastards did quite the number on you. I could see that your leg was swollen. So, I gave you a special herb I invented. It's a painkiller. Works as good as morphine, only not so addictive."

"An herb?"

"I've studied medicine most of my life," Carlos said. "The word is doctor."

"I know what a doctor is," Pearce said. "Those herbs are valuable. You ought to store them for yourself. Why waste them on a stranger?"

"Waste?" Carlos said. There was a sternness in his voice. "I don't consider a human life *waste.*" He stood up. "Do you?"

Pearce sighed. The small talk showed no signs of ending.

"Sometimes. Maybe most of the time. I'm not sure anymore."

"Why?"

"The world we've created. You don't think it was bad sunburn that wiped out the population, do you?"

"When the Death Flash happened, there were close to eight billion people in the world. It only took a handful to fire the missiles. You think they represent all people?"

Pearce didn't answer. He pocketed his few remaining items and gazed out the window. He noticed the old man watching intently. He stood up, as though having received a large burst of energy.

"What do you see?"

"Hmm?" Pearce shook his head. "Oh, nothing. I just wanted to make sure none of those gang members were around. It's uh…been a long day."

"Yes, it has," Carlos agreed. "Apologies—I thought you saw somebody out there. I'm waiting for someone to arrive."

"Waiting?" Pearce said.

"I have another daughter and a son. Good people, they've started a community. They built a water spring, if you can believe it!" Carlos was smiling. "They've always wanted me to join them out there, but I guess I'm a little too focused on trying to restore this old wasteland." That smile quickly disappeared. "Now, I regret not being there. Me being here has caused them to trek through this area to get to me. I have a grandson…"

"Is that so?" Pearce said.

"His name's Paul. He's a really good boy. Very kindhearted, but very tough for a kid. I think those are qualities that need to be instilled on young men, as well as integrity. Oh, forgive me, I'm getting preachy now."

"Hope his pop's been teaching him how to use a gun and knife. Around here, he'll be bug food."

"Oh, his father means well," Carlos said. "I do think he leans a little *too* hard on the harmonious way of life. I guess he's overcompensating for the boy's mother abandoning them." He forced a chuckle, giving Pearce the impression he was holding back feelings of distress. "Don't get me wrong, Mr. Pearce, just because I believe in the good of mankind, doesn't make me oblivious to the evils that lurk. Trust me, I know all about them."

Pearce nodded, his mind flashing back to the raid.

"I believe you."

"I suppose it doesn't make a difference." Carlos wiped a tear from his eye. "Eh, Paul's sick. Bit by a spider. I examined the specimen. The venom isn't the problem—it's the infection they carry. It needs to be caught in its early stages. I've treated people with similar bites. Those infections are worse than the mutations that lurk in this valley." He sighed. "Graf waited too long. Not his fault—he's no doctor. Even if they made it here, it would be too late; the infection would've run its course by now. If I was there and not so occupied with this valley, I might've been able to save him."

"You live out here. Haven't you found the Red Flower? Wouldn't that work on him?" Pearce said.

"Possibly, if the legends are true," Carlos said. "But I've never found one. I've looked, but it seemed I'm always being tricked by those damned red dandelions."

Pearce nodded. *I know what you mean.*

"Is that why you're out here? Hoping to cure that Blood Virus?"

"One can only hope," Pearce said.

"Then sir, I wish you a prosperous journey. Just be careful. There's all kinds of dangers out there." He sighed. "I'm worried Star and Graf ran into trouble. I expected them to be here by now." Carlos glanced out the window, wishing he could see his family approaching in the horizon. "All I want is for my kids to arrive safe, and for Paul to get one more hug from his grandpa before…" he looked away, his voice trailing off. "He loves hugs."

"He most certainly does," Pearce said, softly.

CHAPTER 22

The bikers' skin had turned black, covered by an army of ants that fed from their flesh. When Pearce found them, their faces were gone, their muscle tissue exposed.

He looted their pockets and belts, finding a nine-millimeter pistol with two extra magazines and an assault rifle. He found the knife they threatened to mutilate him with. It had a ten-inch blade, the reverse edge serrated. It was a perfect replacement for the one he had lost recently. He continued looting through their vests, shaking the ants off his hands as he pulled a few matches, a tin of chewing tobacco, and a piece of paper.

At first, he assumed the paper was used to roll the tobacco into cigarettes. His first instinct was to chuck it away. He started crumpling it to toss it aside, only to notice the illustration on the other side. Penciled on the paper was a detailed map of Tidal Valley, with X's marked for their campsites. This was likely designed specifically for their scouts, so they knew where to regroup with the gang.

Pearce inspected the motorcycles. Under the seats was a storage compartment. Inside one was a spare pistol, fully loaded with an extra magazine and holster. Pearce strapped both pistols to his belt, wearing one at each hip. He checked the other motorcycle compartment. Inside was a stack of dynamite, containing over a dozen sticks.

In his pocket was Paul's lighter. Pearce pulled it out and gazed at it, then back at the map. He studied the X's on the north side of the cliff, discovering one nearly two miles from the approximate location of the fort.

That's where I'd go if I wanted to regroup.

As Pearce stared at the mark, his mind reflected on the family, particularly the boy. The old man's words of love for his children and grandson echoed in his ears, as clear as though he were standing right beside him. A war waged in his mind between his natural instinct for self-preservation and this strange inner feeling of morality.

All I have to do is find that overturned buggy. The Dirt Diamonds likely haven't bothered to ransack it. They just wanted Star and Graf. If so, then the pack is still there. All I have to do is find it and give myself the Red Flower. After that, I can ride out of here on this motorcycle, and the gang will never know I survived.

Yet, there was a sullen feeling about following this action. Never before had he thought so much about someone else. He hadn't needed to. Perhaps it was because somebody saved him; somebody whom he had refused to help when in need.

Pearce had killed many people in his time. He never counted; he never needed to. Nor had he counted the people he had saved. Because there were none.

"Son of a bitch," he cursed, followed by an exasperated sigh. He glanced at the dynamite.

Not enough to take on forty or fifty Dirt Diamonds. Then again...

An idea sparked in his mind. The inner voice of self-preservation screamed at him.

No, idiot! It'll swallow you up the first chance it gets.

His newly found conscience was quick to respond; *You have the bike. You can keep out of range.*

"Fuck it," he said aloud, ending the silent argument. He placed the dynamite and map back in the storage compartment, then started the engine. He completed a turn then raced as fast as he could to find his way up the cliff.

CHAPTER 23

Star awoke with a splitting headache. She was on the ground, her hands up above her head, tied to an X-shaped post made of wood. Memories of the chase streaked through her mind, instantly reminding her of the situation. She thrashed her feet wildly and pulled down against her binds to no avail.

Her first thoughts were of Paul and Graf. She immediately saw Paul sitting to her left, tied to a post identical to hers. The veins in his neck and face were increasingly discolored. Paul was visibly fatigued, though still highly alert due to the adrenaline. To her left was Graf. He was awake, bellowing curses at the Dirt Diamonds.

Star looked down at herself. Her clothes were untampered with, meaning she hadn't been taken advantage of while unconscious. Monsters like these didn't bother redressing the victims they raped.

Tied down as well, Graf was defenseless except for his words. He was like a dog barking at a pack of hungry wolves.

"I swear, there's a mean fate coming for all of you," he said. "Just remember, there were over TWICE as many of you as there are now. And you're going to die as brutally as they did!"

"Shut up," Star whispered to him. Graf looked over, his face red with fear.

"We're not gonna tell them anything," he said. "We can't. You know what'll happen if they find our spring."

Star nodded. She sucked in a deep breath to calm herself, then took in the world around her. There were between forty and fifty Dirt Diamonds moving about. Four buggies remained as well as three pickup trucks and a couple of motorcycles.

In the middle of the camp was a pit. Several of the raiders were dangling wire over the ledge. Star could hear the hissing sounds below, then realized they were fishing from a lizard pit.

"Shit," she muttered to herself. Near the pit was a small metal cage. They weren't catching lizards for food, but as a means of torture.

Cedoz walked around the pit and approached the three captives. His face and arms were marked from the clash with Pearce, yet, he didn't show any discomfort. His face wrinkled as a smile formed under that mask.

"What I love about Tidal Valley is that we don't usually have to get too creative when extracting important information. Back in the Yipsi Glades, on the coast, over in Scada Valley, we usually have to resort to cutting off fingers, stoning people slowly, draw-and-quarter techniques, things like that. But here, the land has presented us plenty of new ways of doing things, and more effectively too." He stood over Paul, who looked him in the eye. "You afraid, boy?"

Paul glared at him, his bound hands forming fists. Then, slowly, his middle fingers lifted out from the clenches.

"You're a rare specimen," Cedoz said. He looked at Star and Graf. "You should be proud."

"Don't you touch him," Graf said.

"I'd rather not," Cedoz said. "Boy looks riddled with disease. I think we'll try another method first." The raiders behind him struggled as they fished out a violent lizard from the pit. The toothed reptilian thrashed as they dangled it over the ledge, then slipped it into the cage and locked it. It clawed at the grate, scraping it with its teeth and claws.

"Is that your new pet?" Graf remarked.

"Why…yes," Cedoz said. "Why don't you pet it?" The leader stepped behind his post, along with two of his raiders who carried the cage. It shook viciously as the lizard attacked every inch of the grate.

"The fuck you think you're doing?" Graf said. He started to wiggle uncomfortably, looking over his shoulder at the Dirt Diamonds. Slowly, they raised the cage near to his hands.

"Letting you pet my new lizard," Cedoz said. He grabbed Graf's wrist and pried the fingers from the clenched fist. "Do you object?"

"Yeah, I prefer cats. Specifically, normal, not mutated ones," Graf said.

"I see," Cedoz said. "Unfortunately, this poor lizard here takes great offense to that. Seeing as we're in *his* neighborhood, I'll have to see to it that you give him the attention he wants. Unless," his grip tightened as he leaned in closer, "you tell me where you've discovered your water."

"Water? What water?" Graf said. Cedoz shook his head.

"After everything that's happened, I was sure you'd be a little prudent." Cedoz held Graf's hand in place, keeping his finger straight as they brought the cage closer to it."

"Get that thing away from me you fuck!" Graf snarled, squirming. The cage closed in. Cedoz guided Graf's finger through the grate. The lizard lunged at the flesh, its mouth chomping rapidly like piranha jaws. Graf thrashed his legs and screamed as needle-like teeth turned his fingertip into minced meat.

The raiders pulled the cage back. The lizard continued attacking the grate, its tongue licking every trace of blood. Graf hyperventilated, his finger throbbing and pumping blood down his arm.

Cedoz kneeled down beside him.

"Tell me what I want to know, or my pet will work its way down to the next knuckle," he said.

Graf shook his head. "Fuck you." Cedoz glanced at Star.

"What about you? You gonna tell me where your water comes from?"

Star looked at him, then at her brother. Graf shook his head, mouthing *Don't say anything.*

"Water?" Star said. "What water?"

"Alright. Have it your way." Cedoz stood up and forced Graf's hand open again. The prisoner shook as he heard the raiders move closer with the cage.

"Go kiss a Komodo, you mangy bast—AGHHH!" The lizard ravaged his index finger, shredding every bit of skin and muscle down through the middle knuckle.

CHAPTER 24

What am I doing?

The question repeated itself in Pearce's mind as he arrived at the hatch where he and the family escaped the tunnel. First, he completed a brief sweep of the surrounding area to make sure there were no Dirt Diamonds or other thugs nearby. After confirming he was alone, he parked the motorcycle two hundred feet from the hatch, then removed the dynamite from the storage.

He took another glance at the map, memorizing the path he would have to take. Once he got moving again, he would not have the luxury of stopping. The bike was already positioned east, which was where he would need to go.

Crumpling the paper in his hands, he took the dynamite and lighter to the hatch. Already, he could feel mild vibrations under his feet. Something was moving in the tunnels, already confirming the presence of the Fire Lizard. He cautiously lifted the hatch, ready to jump back in case the creature decided to spit fire at him.

The sun reflected on one of its horns below. It was white, as were its teeth, contrasting sharply from its hard, scaly hide. It snarled and attacked the beam of sunlight that poured into the juncture. Even the sun was not allowed to invade its fortress.

"Then you're *really* about to be pissed," Pearce said. He lowered himself down the hatch and descended a few feet, while keeping an eye on the beast. He found a breach in the steel panel, exposing a loose area of dirt. He shoved the stack of dynamite into the hole and pressed it until it was all the way in.

The creature hissed under him, then roared. Pearce glanced down at it, then pulled Paul's lighter.

"Sorry to bother ya, but I need your help," he said. He lit the end of the twelve-inch fuse then bolted out of the hatch. He dashed for the motorcycle and started the engine.

The fuse burnt away, igniting the dynamite. A dynamic explosion launched a wave of rock and soil upward. The beast shrieked madly. Its ears rang and eyes stung from dust and smoke. Bits of rock and metal rained down on the surrounding landscape, revealing a widened entryway.

Pearce waited, listening to the thrashing sounds of the Fire Lizard. A tornado of fire burst from the hole in the earth. The creature clawed its way out, its mouth and neck bleeding from the explosion. After fully emerging, it stumbled like a bat, its senses having been rattled from the blast.

It stumbled out of the smoke cloud, allowing the sun to expose its bodily features previously obscured by the dark. Its legs were long and cat-like, with long curved claws at the end of them. A line of spikes lined the creature's back from its head all the way to its clubbed tail.

"Come on," Pearce said, revving his engine. The beast turned itself around repeatedly, its eyes shut tight. It expelled puffs of fire and lashed its tail blindly. Pearce groaned impatiently and revved his engine to get its attention. It turned its head, its eyes gradually opening. "Okay, enough with the bullshit. You gonna eat me or not?" He drew a pistol and fired several shots at the creature's head.

Suddenly, it came alive, roaring vehemently. Its long legs struck the ground as it scampered toward its meal.

Pearce accelerated, right as a gust of fire swept near him. Veering wide of the crumpled buildings, Pearce kept out of range of the fire. The creature gave chase, crashing through brick as it smashed through the remnants of the community.

The creature moved faster than he anticipated, forcing Pearce to drive at top speed as he led it east.

"Keep coming," he said. "Keep getting pissed."

CHAPTER 25

Graf screamed as the lizard worked its way through a second finger. The lizard, now covered in his blood, thrashed violently as it sawed through the meat. Cedoz stepped aside, allowing his raiders to continue the torture as he watched with his arms crossed.

"Tell me what you know, and I'll make the pain stop," he said. He motioned for the raiders to halt. They stepped back with the cage, leaving Graf's mangled fingers dangling from the knuckles. One of the raiders pressed a piece of cloth to the wounds while another tied some nylon laces to reduce the bleeding. Cedoz waited, allowing Graf a few moments to get his wits back. His head nodded back and his eyes closed. One of the raiders drove a stick into his exposed knuckles, the sudden shock zapping Graf like a bolt of lightning. He yelled out, fully awakened and alert.

"Don't be dozing off when I'm talking to you. It's not polite," Cedoz warned. He grabbed a fistful of Graf's hair and pulled his head close. "Where's the water? Where'd you come from?"

"North Pass," Graf lied, gasping with each word. "There's a camp. Thirty-five miles northwest of here."

Cedoz released his grip then stood up. He glared at his prisoner, then at the boy.

"Come on," Star said. "He told you where the water's at. Let us go."

"You're in no position to make demands of me," Cedoz said. "Besides, I don't take well to being told lies."

"What? But I told you…"

Cedoz grabbed Graf by the throat, cutting him off.

"You lied," he said. "We saw your wagon. You were coming from the northeast, not the northwest."

"We had to get around some steep hills," Graf spat.

"Now you lied again," Cedoz said. He shoved Graf back against the post. The raiders behind Graf moved in with the lizard. "No," Cedoz said, holding a hand up. "Physical torture of the body won't do it for this one. To get what we want, we must ravage his spirit. Throw the boy in the pit."

Graf lurched against the post.

"NO!"

"It's your punishment for thinking me a fool," Cedoz said. Graf struggled fruitlessly as two raiders approached Paul. His face was pale, his breathing labored. The raiders looked at the sick boy, noticing his fragile condition, then back at Cedoz.

"He looks like he's about to die anyway, my lord," one of them said.

"Then we will grant him mercy from his slow fate," Cedoz said, "by throwing him in the pit."

"Yes, my lord." The raiders removed the bindings and lifted the boy off the ground. "Hopefully, the lizards won't catch what he had." The raiders laughed, not noticing the boy's hand slipping into his back pocket.

The ploy had worked. Feeling ill in reality, it didn't take much imagination for Paul to put on the façade of a kid moments away from death. The raiders held him by the shoulders and dragged him toward the pit.

Like a possessed spirit, Paul came alive, whipping the locket like a miniature lasso. The pointed picture frame struck each of them in the eye, the sudden pain causing them to let go.

"Go, Paul! Go!" Graf shouted. The boy turned around and ran, winding around another raider who attempted to intercept.

"You incompetent baboons, get that little weasel!" Cedoz yelled. His raiders took off in pursuit, running past Star. Twisting her body, she stuck her legs out, tripping both men. She then kicked as hard as she could, catching one of them in the mouth with her boot.

Cedoz grabbed her by the throat and lifted her off the ground. Star gagged, eyes wide open as his grip tightened. Cedoz looked past her as three of his men chased Paul into the distance. Though the boy was sick, he was still fast.

"I can assure you of one thing, woman," Cedoz said. He pried the bindings from the post, keeping her wrists tied together. "You will live a long life, I promise you that. You will be my slave, forever. You will be a Dirt Diamond. But first, you will watch the boy's flesh be stripped from his bones, followed by your man. In the meantime, I will allow my use for you to begin." He threw her to the ground, right at the feet of a group of eager Dirt Diamonds. They looked at her with lustful eyes, then glanced back at Cedoz for permission. After receiving a nod of approval, they descended on her.

****

Pearce felt the heat of magma-hot fire breath that whooshed behind him. It was the creature's fourth attempt to incinerate him. Each time, Pearce managed to keep a few feet out of range, aggravating the beast further. It followed him across the wasteland, keeping pace with the bike. It whipped its tail as it ran, the club smashing new craters into the ground.

Pearce watched the sun to make sure he was moving in the right direction. The chase had gone on for at least two miles, and the beast showed no signs of letting up.

That damn camp better be here somewhere, or else this was a really stupid idea.

He heard a deep growl from the Fire Lizard behind him. A gulping sound followed, indicating it was going to spit another stream of flame. He zagged to the left after hearing the third *gulp* sound. The fire rippled past him, nearly singeing his leg and tires.

The creature had gained distance on him, putting him in range of its breath. Pearce continued to veer, only to find himself on a collision course with a line of rocks. They were as large as cars, separated by a few feet. Pearce drove the bike in a curving path, winding between two car-sized boulders.

The lizard ceased its fire breath and continued after its prey. It swung its tail, smashing one of the boulders in half. Shards of rock struck Pearce's back, causing him to glance back. The creature crawled over the rubble that was once a boulder and continued to gallop after him.

Pearce looked back, just in time to see the enormous sandpit directly in front, sixteen feet in width, indicating an arachnid of nearly twenty feet waited inside.

"Christ!"

He swerved to the right, the wheels kicking dirt and rocks into the loose sand. He curved around the pit and steered to the right. The Fire Lizard bellowed as it nearly took a nosedive into the pit. It threw its weight to the side, shifting its momentum to follow the human.

The sand swirled, the beast within disturbed. The creature slowly emerged, only to find that its potential prey had already fled. Thus, it sank back beneath the loose sand and waited.

Pearce went straight, cutting through a dried riverbank. He descended the small slope then pushed his acceleration to the max when climbing the opposite side. He cleared the edge with an arching jump and stuck the landing.

Looking directly ahead, he saw a barren landscape dotted with red dandelions and rocks. Moving between them was a child being chased by three men wearing chains.

Paul had felt the fatigue after only a couple hundred feet. Despite this, he continued pushing himself. Succumbing to the spider venom was a preferable choice compared to being eaten alive by lizards.

His chest ached and his muscles grew sore. His lungs felt as though they were being torn apart from within. There was a flaming pain in his kidneys, which were now starting to shut down. Paul couldn't go on any longer. He hit his knees and fell to the ground.

"Nice try, you little rat," one of the raiders said. They encircled the boy, each one sporting a devilish smile.

"Why ya running, kid? Didn't you know you were invited to supper?" All three of them bellowed with laughter.

A deafening roar brought their amusement to a cold end. They looked to the horizon, seeing the four-legged reptilian rampaging their way. Those smiles changed into expressions of pure terror. They quickly backtracked, not even noticing the motorcycle that sped near them.

Paul looked up, hearing the screeching stop near his head, and saw Pearce.

"Every time I see you, you're always knee deep in trouble," he said. He grabbed the boy and pulled him up onto the seat, then sped out of the creature's way.

The beast nearly turned to go after the bike, then noticed three other human targets that were much closer.

The raiders drew their weapons and fired at the creature. It charged, its hide deflecting the ineffective projectiles. It reared its head back and gulped. Two raiders moved sideways, while the third continued shooting. The lizard threw its head forward, releasing a gust of flame that melted his body to ashes.

It moved in on the other two, looking back and forth between each as it decided which to attack first. A gunshot from one to its left concluded its decision. The raider backtracked, yelling maniacally as he repeatedly fired into the beast. With a swift turn of its body, the Fire Lizard swung its tail. Its club connected with the thug's body, smashing him into a shapeless blob of flesh. The Fire Lizard scampered toward the third, its jaws wide. The raider emptied his pistol, then chucked the empty weapon at the approaching beast. He let out one final scream as its jaws descended on him. They chomped down, the spiked teeth punching through his body. The creature munched, pulping his body until it was slurped into its gullet.

Pearce circled the beast with the motorcycle. He pulled out one of his pistols and handed it back to Paul.

"Get its attention," he said. Paul, with one hand clinging to Pearce, aimed at the Fire Lizard, then fired repeatedly. The beast lifted its head, pinpointing the sound of gunfire, then spotted them. With an ear-piercing screech, it came at them. Razor claws ripped at the dirt with each step, its throat gulping to generate another breath of fire.

"Which way's the camp?" Pearce asked. Paul pointed the direction, then held on tight as Pearce led the beast to its next site of destruction.

****

Star swung her hands, catching one of her attackers in the jaw. Rolling on her back, she thrust a kick out, catching another in the groin.

"Get away from her!" Graf shouted. He struggled to free himself from his post to no avail. The raiders piled down on Star like a pack of wolves. She struggled, kicking another in the jaw until finally a duo of them managed to pin her legs down. She struck another with an elbow before another one pinned her arms behind her head.

Star groaned, unable to move. A couple of raiders approached, then proceeded to have a shoving match to decide who would have the first go at her. She shook as a third moved his hands along the waistband of her pants. He took a knife, ready to cut away her clothing.

A pounding noise brought pause to the entire camp. Something large was approaching. They looked back, then dispersed in panic.

Cedoz turned to look, and in a rare display of fear, he ran as the beast charged into the camp.

The gang departed from Star and ran to their vehicles, collecting weapons and ammo to fight the beast. Star leapt to her feet and threw her arms at the thug with the knife as he started to run. She pulled her binds down over his neck, choking him.

The thug struggled, wildly thrashing the knife but missing. Star pulled tighter. With one final spasm, the thug lost consciousness. She took the knife and cut the rope from her wrists, then ran to Graf.

"Shoot it! Get in the vehicles!" Cedoz shouted to his gang. Gunshots filled the air as bullets struck the lizard. It smashed through the center of the camp, swatting thugs left and right with its arms. Claws sliced flesh, spilling blood and entrails onto the ground. It swung its tail high, then brought it downward like a hammer. The club connected with a thug's head, smashing his body into a crater.

Pearce circled the camp and watched as the Fire Lizard wreaked havoc on the Dirt Diamonds. He found a large boulder and stopped.

"Hide here," he told Paul. The boy got off the bike and crouched behind the boulder. He was watching the carnage, his face expressing concern. Pearce knew what he was thinking. "I'm gonna get your folks. Just hang tight. Use that if you need to." He pointed at the pistol in his hands. Paul nodded and backed out of sight, clutching the weapon with both hands.

Pearce raced the motorcycle into the camp, drawing his remaining pistol as he neared. Off to the side was a pickup truck with several stacks of dynamite. Several raiders approached it, collecting ammo and bazookas. Pearce aimed his pistol and fired into the bed of the pickup. One of the bullets struck a dynamite stick. A tremendous explosion followed, tossing several bodies through the air.

With his rifle in hand, Pearce jumped off his bike and took aim. The explosion caused several raiders to scatter, giving him plenty of targets to shoot at. Up ahead to the left, one of them pointed at him and shouted.

"THERE!"

It was his last word, before a bullet punched through his skull. Pearce double-tapped, killing another. He flipped the lever into full auto, then unleashed the full fury of the weapon. Bullets struck numerous thugs, spraying blood through entry and exit wounds. Pearce quickly reloaded, then scooped up another rifle from a dead raider. Dual wielding the rifles in his muscular arms, Pearce blasted into the crowd.

Across the camp, the Fire Lizard thrashed its tail, pulverizing one of the buggies and its four occupants with its club. Metal, stained with human blood, rained through the camp. The beast moved inward, unfazed by the hundreds of rifle rounds that struck it.

The buggy with the M60 drove near, its gunner shooting for the creature's head. The beast twitched its head, annoyed by the constant pelting from projectiles. It gulped, then spat its hellish breath. Fire consumed the vehicle, inducing screams from the men inside. The flames ignited the gunpower within the munitions, causing rounds to zip in numerous different directions. The driver twisted the wheel illogically as he was burned alive, driving over a couple of his companions in the process.

The burning buggy struck a pickup truck, the flames igniting the fuel tank. In a tremendous *BOOM*, both vehicles exploded.

The beast swung its tail and struck another raider, the impact causing his body to burst. It gulped again and turned at a group of raiders who fired at it with assault rifles. A river of fire engulfed them, causing the group of four to run wildly for several seconds before the flames ate through their bodies.

Cedoz gripped his double-barrel shotgun and aimed for the beast's head, then discharged both barrels. The blasts did nothing except gain its attention. It looked his way and snarled. Cedoz ejected his empty cartridges and tried to reload. The beast approached, then pivoted on its legs. Cedoz saw the tail whipping toward him. He dove to the ground, the club passing over him. Abandoning the lost shotgun, he jumped to his feet and ran.

Up ahead was a motorcycle being boarded by one of his raiders. Cedoz could hear the creature chasing after him. Its breath grew hot as it narrowed the gap. Cedoz drew his 500. Magnum and shot the raider in the knee. The man fell, his leg mangled as though hit by a rocket. As he squirmed in agony, Cedoz jumped on the bike and took off. The beast abandoned its chase in favor of the helpless raider. It scooped him up in its jaws and shook its head, shredding the man to bits.

Star cut the binds from Graf's wrists. His fingers were still bleeding profusely from the lizard's bites.

"Stay awake," she said.

"I'm good," Graf groaned. He held his injured hand in his lap while Star took the laces from the boot of a dead raider and tied it around his arm to slow the circulation.

"Look out," Graf said, looking behind her. Star turned and froze, seeing the muzzle of a rifle pointed at her head. The Dirt Diamond holding it snarled and began to squeeze the trigger.

A gunshot rang out. Star shook in fright, then watched as the raider's corpse fell to the ground, his face imploded by a rifle round. She looked up as Pearce ran up to them. He fired the two rifles, spraying bullets into a grouping of Dirt Diamonds. Bodies spun and fell, while others charged forward.

Pearce continued firing back until both weapons ran dry.

"Get out of here," he said, discarding the rifles. Drawing his pistol, he returned fire, striking another thug in the head. Star grabbed Graf and helped him to his feet, leading him away from the carnage while Pearce engaged the raiders. Pearce shot another, exploding the man's throat. Another round found its way through the stomach of a female raider. The impact shook her body. She looked down, her final moments spent gazing dumbfoundedly at her fatal wound.

Four more Dirt Diamonds advanced, firing pistols and shotguns at him. Pearce dove behind a burning truck and reloaded his pistol. The raiders resumed firing, hoping for a lucky round to pierce through the barrier and hit their target. Pearce adjusted into a kneeling position, keeping himself obscured behind the burning truck and buggy. He peeked around the corner and fired a few rounds. Several bullets zipped in his direction. Suddenly, the pistol was flung from his hand. It landed several feet away, the slide bent into an otherworldly position. A rifle round had struck it just above the grip.

The raiders closed in for the kill. One moved around the burning vehicle, his shotgun ready at the shoulder. He lined Pearce up for the kill, seeing him crouched with an arm drawn back over his head. In that hand was a knife.

Pearce flung the knife, embedding its blade into the raider's throat. The raider spun, his hands dropping the weapon and going for his throat. Pearce sprinted and grabbed him by the shoulders, putting him between himself and the other three thugs as they opened fire. Several rounds struck the human shield in the chest.

The shooting stopped as each weapon ran dry. Pearce seized the opportunity and rushed the group. He struck one in the jaw with his elbow, knocking him to the ground. The second drew a knife and lunged for Pearce's neck. Pearce caught him by the wrist and twisted hard, bending the joint past its capability. Flattening his hand, he chopped the raider in the throat, imploding his airway. The third drew a knife and moved in. Pearce grabbed the weakened thug and swung him in the way. The knife plunged into the unlucky raider's stomach, widening his already gasping mouth in agony.

The knife-wielding raider yanked his weapon free and knocked his now-dead comrade out of the way. He slashed repeatedly, hoping to carve the warrior open. Each miss enraged him further, causing his attack to grow sloppy.

Pearce snapped a jab into his nose, knocking him back. The raider, now bleeding, lunged with the knife. In doing so, he unwittingly walked right into a kick to the ribs. He felt the bones snap and plunge into his lungs. He fell to his knees, eyes wide before faceplanting into the dirt.

Pearce turned around as the last remaining thug picked himself off the ground. The man briefly rubbed his jaw, then rushed Pearce with fists raised high. He threw a punch, missed, then kicked, only for Pearce to block it in a hammering motion with his fist. Pearce retaliated with a punch to the jaw, then another to the stomach. The raider swung a wild haymaker, missing his opponent entirely and opening himself up to a kick in the face. He staggered, bleeding from the nose and mouth. Yelling crazily, he threw another wide haymaker. Pearce caught his arm then, using his momentum, threw the raider over his shoulder. The Dirt Diamond hit the ground and rolled…right into the lizard pit.

The reptiles converged on him, shredding his flesh with rapid bites.

Pearce looked around, seeing the camp in utter dismay. The Fire Lizard was thirty yards away, scorching another raider in its heat blast. It scampered past his smoldering body to pursue three others. They cowered behind one last remaining buggy, shooting at the creature with everything they had. A single swipe of its tail toppled the vehicle over. The tail slashed back, crushing one of the raiders and causing the last two to flee.

And they were truly the last. As Pearce studied his surroundings, he concluded that there was no more movement. The Dirt Diamonds were dead, their final members moments away from being mauled to death by the ferocious Fire Lizard.

The only movement Pearce saw was in the distance. Two people: Star and Graf, running away from the camp. There was someone else several dozen yards away from them, moving on a motorcycle. Even from this distance, Pearce recognized the mask on Cedoz's face.

There was no way he would reach them in time on foot. Pearce looked around, seeing the burning buggies and pickup trucks…and one remaining motorcycle.

CHAPTER 26

The camp glowed behind them as Star and Graf ran. Graf held his mangled hand close to his chest. What remained of the mauled fingers would have to be amputated. However, he wasn't focused on his injury, but on the whereabouts of his son. The last he saw Paul, he had fled into the wasteland.

"Paul!" he shouted. He looked around frantically. "Paul!"

"Look! There!" Star said, pointing to the southeast. Graf blew a sigh of relief when he saw his son waving at them from behind a boulder.

The sound of a motorcycle engine drew his attention behind him. He turned around, seeing Cedoz speeding directly at them with a revolver in hand.

"Get down!" Graf said, pushing his sister out of the way. Cedoz fired, his shot grazing Graf's shoulder. He fell to one knee, checking himself to see if he'd been hit. Cedoz slowed the bike to a stop and stepped off. Star jumped to her feet and threw a punch into his jaw. Unfazed, he thrust his arm out and grabbed her by the throat.

Graf launched himself at the bandit chief, only to be knocked down by a kick to the chest. Cedoz lifted Star off the ground with effortless ease, then threw her down on top of her brother.

He pointed his revolver down at them. Star rolled off of Graf and started to stand, only to feel the muzzle press against her forehead. She froze, her breathing labored.

"Go ahead," she said. "Shoot."

"I will," Cedoz said. He pointed the revolver away, then pushed her back to the ground with his foot. "But not you; not yet. First, I'm gonna take care of that boy of yours."

"No!" Graf said, leaping to his feet with his fists raised. Cedoz struck him in the face with his revolver, knocking him out cold. He then plowed a fist into Star's stomach, blowing the wind out of her.

As he turned to march for the boy, he heard something approaching. An engine.

The warrior.

He turned and aimed his revolver. The bike was coming directly at him, reared up on its back tire. Several feet away was Pearce, rolling off to the side after jumping clear. The bike plowed into Cedoz, launching him several feet back. The revolver was shaken from his hand as he hit the ground, bouncing several yards away.

Pearce was on his feet and charging the leader.

"Get the boy," he said to Star. Cedoz was already back on his feet, his eyes burning with fury. He clenched his fists and advanced on Pearce. His right arm drew back, and in a laser motion, was launched toward his enemy's face.

Pearce raised both hands in a cross block, deflecting the punch upward. Cedoz plowed a left uppercut into his unguarded midsection, then punched again for the face, this time hitting Pearce in the eye. Cedoz assaulted like a wild beast, his punches sloppy but ferocious. Peace put his guard up, only for a swinging fist to knock both hands to the side, exposing his face for a left hook that landed along his temple.

He staggered back, then sidestepped to avoid another barrage of punches. Cedoz turned and threw a kick, catching the warrior in the left ribs. Pearce reeled backward. As soon as he hit the ground, Cedoz had advanced. He was standing over him with his foot raised, ready to stomp Pearce's face into the ground.

Pearce rolled to his right, the boot crashing inches from his head. Cedoz pivoted and kicked him in the stomach, rolling Pearce like a log. He kicked again, bashing the loner's ribs.

Star slapped Graf in the face repeatedly.

"Wake up, you stupid shit!" She slapped him again. Graf stirred. Suddenly, realizing where he was and the situation, he snapped back to life.

"Paul! Where's Paul?"

"He's safe," Star said. "We have to go. He's over…" she looked to the boulders, only to realize Paul wasn't there. "What the—"

There he was, running toward them. Star's heart fluttered. He wasn't running toward them…but Cedoz.

"No! Paul! Go back!"

Cedoz grabbed Pearce by the vest and lifted him up, headbutted him in the face, then kneed him in the stomach. Pearce struggled in a vain attempt to pry his grip off of him, only to be struck again in the face. Cedoz struck with another knee to the gut, doubling Pearce over, then slammed an elbow into the back of his neck. Pearce fell flat on the ground, his entire body surging with pain.

To make matters worse, his lungs were enflaming. He coughed violently, spitting blood into the dirt.

Damn blood virus!

Cedoz grabbed him again and pulled up, arching his back. He wrapped his arm around his neck and squeezed tightly.

Pearce struggled. He pressed his feet to the ground, balancing himself. With both hands, he tried futilely to loosen the leader's grip. Cedoz squeezed his arm tighter. Pearce's face had turned purple, much to Cedoz's delight.

"Time to die," he said. He arched his back, lifting Pearce off his feet.

Pearce gritted his teeth, unable to breathe. He hung from his neck, his vision quickly clouding.

He could see Cedoz's face in the corner of his eye, his cheeks wrinkling around the mask, exposing the edges of the infected flesh beneath.

With all his might, Pearce reached past his head and grabbed at the mask. His fingers slipped under the edge. The nerves in Cedoz's face lit up, causing his grip to loosen slightly.

Pearce rammed an elbow back into Cedoz's stomach. Tucking his chin down, he slipped out of the chokehold. His lungs welcomed the warm air as he sucked in a deep breath.

Cedoz quickly adjusted his mask, then turned to face Pearce. Enraged, he swung wildly. The first blow caught Pearce in the jaw, knocking him back. A second one missed entirely, as did the third. Frustrated, Cedoz kicked, only for a downward block to redirect his leg and knock him off balance.

Pearce pivoted, completing a full three-sixty-degree rotation, swinging a kick in a hooking motion. The heel crashed into Cedoz's jaw, catching him by surprise. Staggered by the blow, he faltered, his guard dropped. Pearce kicked again, connecting the top of his foot with the leader's left temple. Sweat and dirt exploded from Cedoz's face as the impact rocked his head. Pearce rotated again, this time thrusting a straight side kick square into his chest. It was like being hit with a battering ram. Cedoz finally fell backward, his body vibrating visibly as he hit the ground.

Growling in frustration, the leader stood back up and charged again. Pearce leaned to the side, dodging a punch to the head. He raised his arms, blocking a haymaker, then countered with an elbow to the mouth. Cedoz faltered, his hands moving toward his mask. Pearce pressed the attack, landing an uppercut to the chin. A right hook followed, driving Cedoz back further. The leader swung back, striking Pearce with a punch to the face.

Pearce absorbed the blow but continued to advance. He struck with a kick to the chest, then punched the leader again in the mouth.

Blood was now seeping from the edges of the mask. Cedoz looked at his hands, seeing the red that covered his skin. The sight of his own blood fueled his rage. He raised a hand as Pearce punched again, catching his fist in his palm. The two men struggled, each attempting to outmuscle the other.

Pearce was shaking, unable to free his fist from the leader's grasp. Then, as quickly as flipping a switch, all energy vanished from his body. Cedoz kicked low, striking Pearce in his injured leg, igniting the nerves.

Pearce bared teeth in agony as he collapsed. Cedoz stomped down, hitting the fractured area again.

"You've failed," the leader said. "You're going to die now. And when I'm through with you, that boy is next. I will twist his little head around like a corkscrew. Then I'll kill his father. And the woman, she'll be my new bride. The first member of my new band of Dirt Diamonds."

"Don't expect her to kiss you on the lips," Pearce quipped. Cedoz kicked him again, this time in the stomach. Pearce rolled over, coughing up drops of blood. He rolled onto his stomach, then looked up ahead. Several feet away from him was a plant. He recognized the green leaves, long narrow stem connecting to its red head. A red dandelion.

Cedoz pressed a knee on Pearce's back. With both hands, he grabbed him by the jaw and back of his head, ready to snap his neck. Before he could, Pearce rolled, throwing a hand into the leader's face. His fingers caught the edge of his mask and pulled, ripping it free from his face. The air made contact with the infected jaw, firing up nerves like city lights. His lower jaw was skeletal, his cheeks nearly gone entirely.

Pearce plucked the red dandelion and shoved it into the leader's jaw. For the first time in years, Cedoz shrieked in agonizing pain. The needles embedded themselves in the soft flesh, shooting poison through his veins. Cedoz jumped off of Pearce and stumbled backward. He spit the dandelion out, then clutched his face with both hands. His hands then moved to his throat, as the infection caused his airway to enflame.

He sucked at the air, desperate to get a breath. He shrieked madly, his malformed jaw biting at the air. The veins bulged in his neck and face, darkening in color. Cedoz fell to his knees, clutching his throat. He glared vengefully at his enemy, who was now standing upright and watching him die. Cedoz reached, desperate for one final attempt to strangle Pearce and take him to the grave with him.

"Now you can start a new gang… in hell," Pearce said. He struck the leader with a kick to the face, driving him backward. Cedoz sprawled out on the ground, glaring up at the sky as the life faded from his body.

CHAPTER 27

The Fire Lizard snapped its jaws, impaling the raider with its teeth. It chomped repeatedly, mashing his body into pulp then swallowing. It felt the stinging sensation of shotgun pellets crashing against its throat. The beast glanced down at the final raider, who was frantically backing away, pumping the shotgun until each shell was spent.

The lizard unleashed its fiery breath onto the tiny opponent. The raider shrieked in agony, dancing back and forth in flames before succumbing to his death. The Fire Lizard turned around and gazed at the camp in search of any remaining human foes. There was no movement around it aside from dancing flames. The beast lingered, feeling a desire to find itself a new tunnel and finish out its slumber.

The sound of struggle drew its attention to the west. The beast moved slowly, its eyes wincing as they endured the sting of sunlight. Then it saw them; five humans, one of which had just collapsed to the ground. Possibly dead. Whether it was or wasn't, there were still four others it needed to slaughter before it could return to its sleep.

Pearce took in several deep breaths as the old man's herbs gradually subsided the pain. Graf hugged his son and sister, relieved to be free from the Dirt Diamond's wrath. They gathered around Pearce and helped him balance on his injured leg.

"I thought you didn't give a shit," Graf said, smiling.

"I don't," Pearce said, pretending not to care.

"Yeah, I call bullshit on that," Star said. Her smile faded as she noticed the huge lizard stepping through the camp's perimeter. Its red eyes gazed at them, its tongue flicking before it let out a triumphant roar.

Graf gulped.

"I don't suppose this was part of your grand plan?"

"No…I didn't quite think this part through," Pearce said. The beast began its charge, snapping its jaws hungrily. A high-pitched shriek filled their eardrums as the group started to run.

"The motorcycles," Pearce said. "Get on the motorcycles." Star and Graf hurried to Cedoz's bike and lifted it onto its wheels. Pearce and Paul boarded the other. "Hang on, boy," he told Paul as he started the engine.

The beast closed in within twenty yards, gulping deep to generate a burst of flame. Both pairs of people sped off, right as a stream of fire singed the ground they recently occupied. The beast snarled, realizing it had missed, and marked the ground in an earth-shaking pursuit.

Pearce and Paul shook in their seat as they rode away. Something was wrong; even in this terrain, the bike shouldn't have been shaking this badly. He leaned over to look at the tires. As he feared, the front one had gone flat, likely a consequence of his ambush on Cedoz.

He veered left, avoiding another stream of fire from the creature.

Realizing they were far ahead of the other bike, Star and Graf glanced back.

"Oh no," Star said. "They're in trouble!" Graf turned the bike in a tight circle.

"Let's get its attention," he said. He completed the turn, pointing the bike directly toward the lizard. It turned its head and gulped again. Its head arched back. Graf recognized the sign and veered left. The flame streaked down, singing the rear tire as he sped out of range.

A loud *POP* shook the motorcycle. Star looked back, seeing the rear tire trailing behind them in shreds. The plan had worked, having drawn the creature away from Pearce and Paul. It had also backfired. Now they were in the same predicament.

The beast was getting close. Graf could hear the footsteps as they grew louder. He saw the beast in the mirror, its face taking up the entire sheet of glass. It sprang off its back legs, reaching forward with its claws. He spun to the side, barely keeping the motorcycle upright as the beast landed beside them.

Paul winced as he watched the creature swing its tail. His dad was able to drive the bike out of range, once again avoiding death by the skin of his teeth. Pearce stopped the bike and tried to think of a solution. The beast was not going to give up until they were dead. In addition, he had no weapons to fight it with; not that bullets were of any use anyway. The artillery had been blown up back at the Dirt Diamonds' camp.

Pearce's mind raced. *God, the only thing I can think of is possibly lead it toward the cliff and HOPE that I can trick it into falling off. Of course, the damn ledge is a couple miles away at least. We'll be scorched to death or eaten before we make it there. If only there was something closer I could use to trap it...*"

"The sandpit," he said aloud. Paul held on tight as Pearce accelerated to the west. He fought to keep it steady, its flattened tire battering against the ground. Paul coughed, fighting against the fatigue caused by the spider venom. The shaking wasn't helping matters, nor did the sudden dip when Pearce drove through the dried riverbank.

The bike went airborne for a few feet as they came out the other side. Pearce scanned the horizon. There, at his two o'clock, were the line of boulders. Three hundred feet in front of them was the enormous sandpit.

"Alright boy, now you REALLY gotta make sure you're holding on tight," he said. He glanced back at Paul, seeing the confused expression on his face. *Why?* "Because I'm about to do something really stupid."

He sped toward the sandpit and circled along its edges, barely keeping away from the loose soil that comprised it. He completed several passes before the sand began to stir. It swirled like a whirlpool. At the center of the sandy vortex, two enormous black pincers emerged. Pearce steered away as those pincers struck into the hard ground, pulling the massive arachnid out of its hiding place. Huge mandibles twitched over its mouth. Twelve bulb-shaped eyes, black as its shell, stared at the fleshy meals. Its tail coiled, the pointed stinger oozing venom. Eight enormous legs carried it toward the bike, as its pincers opened wide to grab its prize.

Pearce waited for it to get close. Should he get too far away, the beast would give up and return to its lair. He felt his waist tighten as Paul squeezed intensely. The creature reared its arms and cocked its tail, ready to spring forward. Pearce gunned the bike, shooting out of reach. The claws snapped, catching nothing but dirt. The scorpion hissed and darted after them, claws outstretched.

Pearce drove the bike through the riverbank, kicking up pebbles as he emerged out the other side. The arachnid followed, its many legs tearing up waves of gravel as it tore through the riverbank.

"Give me the pistol," Pearce said.

The Fire Lizard pounced again, landing a yard behind the bike. It opened its jaws wide to bite down. Graf jerked the bike to the left, causing the beast to take in a mouthful of dirt.

"Look out!" Star screamed. Graf glanced over his shoulder just in time to see the massive tail swinging at them. Yelling in terror, he tilted the bike to the right, toppling them to the ground. The club passed over the top of them, nicking the handlebars. Star and Graf rolled to their hands and knees. The beast spun with the momentum of its tail, then slowly turned to face them.

"Well…shit," Graf said, accepting his fate. The creature reared its head back, ready to snatch them up.

Pistol shots cracked the air, sending bullets into the lizard's face. The beast turned its head, seeing the second pair of humans approaching. It snarled, ready to engage, only to pause when it saw what followed them.

Graf and Star looked, the latter turning pale as she saw the eight legs carrying the scorpion's twenty-foot body across the wasteland.

"No time for creepy-crawlies," Graf said. "Let's go."

The lizard never noticed them fleeing as it sized up its new foe. Identically, the scorpion abandoned its pursuit of the motorcycle, its eyes now fixed on the new threat directly ahead.

The lizard snarled and the scorpion snapped its claws. It stood poised on its many legs, twitching its tail over its body. Slowly, the two leviathans began to circle.

The lizard threw its head forward and hyperextended its jaws. A river of flame struck the arachnid, singeing its eyes and burning the shell. The arachnid scurried backward, its claws scraping over its smoking face. The lizard began its assault. It came down on it with a bounding leap, landing on the scorpion's back. It bit down on the tail and twisted, its dagger-like teeth penetrating the exoskeleton. Meanwhile, its claws dug into its back, scraping against the segmented body in search of a hollow spot to penetrate.

The scorpion flailed its arms and thrashed its body. Its tail pulled back against those jaws, unable to free itself. It reached high with its pincers and snapped behind its head blindly, unable to get a hold of its opponent. The lizard was standing directly on top of it, its weight driving the arachnid down on its stomach. The lizard whipped its head side-to-side, desperately trying to sever the stinger from the tail. It raised its tail high and brought the club down hard, smashing one of the scorpion's front legs behind the center joint.

Blood spewed from the ruptured exoskeleton, the broken leg spasming uncontrollably as the nerves died. The scorpion stood itself up and rocked to and fro, then spun in circles in an attempt to get the lizard off its back. The reptile continued to scrape against its back, its tail clubbing another leg. The shell snapped like a twig inches from the body and the leg fell off. Blood freefell from the wound like a green waterfall. The lizard pulled harder at the tail, the shell refusing to give way.

Finally, the scorpion teetered onto its side and rolled. The lizard screeched as it lost its balance, its face smashing hard into the ground. It lifted its head and began to stand up, only to feel the sharp pain of jagged claws penetrating its hide. The scorpion had already righted itself and charged, driving the tips of its pincers through the lizard's armored skin like lances. The pincers closed, the edges slicing through the skin. The lizard shrieked, then drove the arachnid back with a breath of flame.

The scorpion flailed its limbs, its claws protecting its eyes. Its legs kicked up a thick cloud of dust that settled over it, extinguishing the flames. Without hesitating, the scorpion charged again, arms outstretched. It stopped just out of reach as the lizard swung its clubbed tail, causing it to miss and expose its back.

Pincers snapped on the tail, the serrated edges cutting deep through the bulletproof skin with ease. The lizard roared and turned to bite at the armored pincers, unable to reach. It swung its body, tearing itself out of the scorpion's reach, losing two large flaps of skin in the process. The two leviathans charged each other and collided. Locked in a terrible embrace, the two beasts tussled, rolling over one another. Legs and arms flailed, jaws and pincers snapped.

Rolling onto its feet, the lizard jumped back, narrowly avoiding a snap of the pincers. The scorpion reared up on its back legs, ready to press the attack. At that moment, the lizard sprang forward, colliding with the beast and tackling it onto its back. Jointed legs thrashed upward as the lizard bit down, prying a section of armor from its underside. It cocked its head back and gulped, ready to roast the exposed flesh with fire. It aimed at the wound and opened its jaws to unleash the flame—right as the scorpion reached with its arms. Both pincers closed around its neck and tightened. Fire roared in the back of the lizard's throat and back into its gullet, unable to pass through the blockage. The only thing the creature could spit was a few useless puffs of hot smoke.

The lizard struggled as the claws cut into its neck. It backed away to free itself, dragging the scorpion along, inadvertently righting its posture in the process. Standing upright, the scorpion pressed forward, bending the lizard's neck with its claws. The lizard twisted in agony, clawing madly as the bug drove it on its side. It flailed its legs, its side bleeding from where it had been gashed.

The pincers released their grip on the neck and snatched both parts of the lizard's jaw. It pressed down, prying the jaw open as it rammed the head into the dirt. The lizard writhed, its range of motion limited without accidentally breaking its own neck. Its nails scraped the scorpion's mouth, ineffective in driving it away.

The tail arched and twitched, then in a lightning fast motion, it vaulted. The stinger plunged into the soft flesh inside. The lizard screamed, then convulsed in pain. Red blood poured from its open mouth as the scorpion wedged its stinger in further. Venom pumped into the bloodstream, putting the lizard into cardiac arrest. The lizard spasmed, then in one final maneuver, broke free from the scorpion's grasp, lacerating its jaws in the process. It stumbled away for several yards, then fell on its chest. Its entire body shook, its arms and tail twitching as though being electrocuted.

It lifted its head, letting out one final roar before the venom took its toll. The beast rolled to its side, its mouth slack.

"Keep back," Pearce said to the family. "Don't draw attention." The group remained quiet and watched as the enormous scorpion slowly approached the dead lizard. Grabbing it by the throat with its claws, it scurried backward, dragging its enormous corpse across the wasteland, back to its lair.

"Okay, I gotta say, what the hell was Dad thinking by living in this place?" Star said.

"God only knows," Graf said. He tore a piece of his shirt off and tightly wrapped around his hand. Paul sat down on the ground, exhausted. His father knelt by him and held him in his lap. "It'll be okay, son." He hated himself for lying, and Pearce could see it in his face. He was looking at a man who was watching his son die.

"He'll be fine," Pearce said.

"What?" Star and Graf looked up. "What do you mean?" Pearce let out a sharp exhale. The instinct of self-preservation fought against his conscience, only to flounder in the end.

"Come with me," he said.

CHAPTER 28

Paul awoke to a stinging sensation in his arm. He was on the ground by the cliff edge where they had fled from the Dirt Diamonds. His father was there by his side, holding his hand.

"It's alright buddy," he said. His eyes were welling with tears. "You just fell asleep."

Paul looked to his other arm. Pearce was kneeled at his other side, slowly driving a syringe into his vein. In the vial was the strange red liquid that he so dearly protected.

Pearce injected the fluid into his arm.

"Don't know who made this claim, but they say the Red Flower is made from the blood of angels," Pearce said. "With their heavenly power, they can heal anything." He finished injecting the fluid. "Not sure if I believe in that sort of thing. But I do believe that you'll be fine."

Paul sat up. Almost immediately, the color was returning to his face. Graf and Star held him tight for several minutes, while Pearce stood to the side. He looked at the empty syringe, then stuffed it into his pack, which he had recovered from the devastated buggy.

"I love you, son," Graf said. Paul hugged him back.

"I love you too, Dad," Paul said back to him.

****

It had been a long two days of rebuilding, but it proved worth it in the end. Carlos applied water to the garden, which had been devastated during the Dirt Diamonds' raid.

"Grandpa!"

Carlos stood up and turned around, wondering if he had heard who he thought. He hurried around to the east side of the house. There, in the distance, his daughter, son, and grandson approached.

He wondered if he was seeing things. By now, his grandson should've been bedridden at best. Yet, here he was, running to him with his arms wide.

"Paul!" Carlos yelled back. He embraced his grandson and lifted him high above his head. "My boy! You…you look…healthy!"

"My friend," Paul said, pointing back to his parents. Carlos looked past Star and Graf. Standing in the distance was the stranger he had helped. They shared a distant gaze, each silently expressing their everlasting respect for each other.

The loner watched as the old man hugged his children and assessed Graf's injuries. Pearce turned away, his deed complete, his new quest now beginning. He had found the Red Flower, and where there was one, there were others. With enough time and patience, he would find another and save himself from the dreadful blood virus.

"Wait!" Pearce turned around, seeing Paul running up to him. The boy threw his hands around the loner and hugged him tight. "You have to go?"

Pearce took a knee.

"I have to. There's something important I have to do," Pearce said. "And you, my friend, have an important job too."

"Shoot more bad guys?"

Pearce bit his lip. "If you have to." He smiled. "Don't tell your grandpa about that."

Paul smiled back at him and nodded.

"But Paul, your job is to take care of your dad, your aunt, and your grandpa. Don't focus on how to kill, but to love."

"Okay," Paul said.

"And Paul?"

"Yeah?"

"You know what the stories say happens to the man touched by the Red Flower?"

"What happens?" Paul asked.

"He lives a long and happy life."

Paul smiled and threw his arms around his friend. Pearce smiled, his heart feeling warm as he hugged him back.

The End

www.ingramcontent.com/pod-product-compliance
Lightning Source LLC
Chambersburg PA
CBHW061242170626

46809CB00007B/2790

9781922323781